Also by Peter Cave and
available from Redemption Books

Mama

Chopper
by Peter Cave

REDEMPTION
BOOKS

First published in the UK
by New English Library, 1971.
This edition published by Redemption Books, 1995.
A divsion of Redemption Films Limited,
BCM PO Box 9235, London WC1N 3XX.

A catalogue record for this book is available
from the British Library.

ISBN 1 899634 05 3

Printed in the UK by
The Guernsey Press Company Limited.
Cover and photographic section printed by
Colin Clapp Printers.

When I was asked to write an introduction to **Redemption's** reprint of *Peter Cave's* cult classics, **Chopper** and **Mama,** I was, I confess, cautious. Why anyone would want to publish, let alone purchase, these tales of bad boy bikers, a quarter of a century on, was a mystery to me.

I didn't dismiss it out of hand, however, I was intrigued and, being of an inquisitive turn of mind, I decided to delve deeper. Rummaging through the attic, I found what I was looking for... a complete collection of biker fiction bearing the *New English Library* logo. Why I've hung on to them, I've no idea. Maybe I'm sentimental. Maybe I thought that, one day, they'd make me some money. But hang on to them I have. As, I suspect, have many of my generation who, though they've moved on a mite since the seventies, can't quite bring themselves to dispence with the trappings of their teens. I flicked through the well-thumbed pages, to familiarise myself with the plot, and found myself stepping back in time, to the days when I knew nothing about bikers, but desired, desperately, to learn.

Chopper appeared in the shops in 1971; *Mama*, twelve months later. Both were best-sellers. Why? The answer is obvious. Look at the covers. Look at the impact they must have had on young, impressionable minds — mine included. Sure the characters are far-fetched. Sure their exploits are exaggerated beyond belief. But, back then, that was what we wanted. And, sad to say, we couldn't get enough of it. We didn't want to be told that the rest of our lives would be taken up with trying to make ends meet; that marriage, mortgage and middle age would follow in swift succession. We wanted to make an impact. We wanted to walk on the wild side. We wanted to take the world by the balls and twist it till it begged for mercy. And if we couldn't break through the barrier, between us and our aspirations, well we'd read about others who had, even if it was mostly a myth.

The novels of *Peter Cave* are as far removed from the reality of the British bike scene as westerns are from the reality of riding the range. The history of the **Hell Angels** owes nothing to flights of fancy. We need no books to tell us how to live our lives. We never have, and we never will. And if anyone imagines, for one fleeting moment, that enlightenment can be found in the pages of paperback pulp, then they've an awful lot to learn. *Chopper* and*Mama* are part of our past only insofar as they were instrumental in shaping the public's perception of us, the *Hells Angels.* Read them, by all means. Enjoy them, for what they are. But remember, the truth is stranger still.

Maz Harris.
Hell Angels MC England.
October 1995

Chopper Harris heard the noise when he was still well over half a mile from the Greek's. The sound of between twenty and thirty powerful motorcycle engines roaring and spitting power at full throttle tended to carry a long way on the night air - despite the thousands of other noises which were an integral part of an overcrowded city.

Even above the roar of his own machine, Chopper picked up the noise and headed towards it as though it were a homing signal.

The sound was unmistakably that of a rev-up...and that could only mean action, of one sort or another.

Action was where Chopper Harris belonged. Like a moth to a naked electric light bulb, or a junkie to his nearest 'fix', a Hells Angel always gravitated towards the nearest possible fight, or the quickest possible sex, or to somewhere an Angel could do something to prove himself one better than an ordinary pig citizen.

Chopper throttled back, causing the engine to belch out a loud backfire from the supercharged carburettor. He pulled into the kerb, jammed the heavy bike up against the pavement and dismounted to make the necessary preparations for whatever the night held in store.

A rev-up meant one of two things; either a burn-up was in the offing, with the chance to risk life and limb for the privilege of showing riding skill and contempt for danger, or the noise was intended to cover up the scene of an impending gang-fight. Blasting motorcycle engines served as a useful and effective camouflage to bury the sounds of breaking bottles, screams of pain and the crunch of breaking, splintering bones.

Either way, Chopper wanted in on the action, and he needed to be ready for it when he arrived.

With slow, deliberate care, he adjusted the side straps of his Nazi stormtrooper helmet. The headpiece was genuine - even having the added prestige value of bearing a bullet scar across the front. It had come, along with the other pieces of Nazi insignia which Chopper wore and cherished, from a small shop in Islington's Camden Passage.

The fact that someone had probably died wearing the helmet often gave Chopper a thrill of pleasure. Perhaps its original wearer had been one of the super-Nazis - a desperate, fanatical and violent young man, fighting for a crazy dream of absolute power and a super-race which could exterminate anyone or anything which stood in its way.

To a Hells Angel, such a dream contained the very essence of what life was all about. Violence and action where were it was at; the reason in itself for existence. The Nazi dream had died, killed off in the face of superior opposition. Now the Angels were the prophets and warriors of a new breed to come. Their code bound them together just as tightly as the Nazi doctrines and propaganda had bound the German people. The urge for dominance and power was the same as it had ever been throughout history; the means of implementing that dominance still remained rooted in violence.

Having tightened the straps to his satisfaction, Chopper adjusted the helmet so that it hung low over his forehead. Even with the padded leather inside, the headgear was virtually useless as a crash-helmet, but it served as a useful defence against fists, bottles and motorcycle chains. It could also take a lot of punishment from heavy, iron-studded bovver boots.

Chopper pulled an old leather gauntlet from under his shirt. The fingers of the glove had been cut off at the level of the first knuckle, and the remainder covered carefully with sharpened metal studs and brass clips. One blow from that glove could peel strips of skin from a victim's face, or blind him with an eyeful of his own blood.

Slipping the fighting glove on his right hand, Chopper flexed his fingers experimentally, adjusting it so that the biggest and sharpest studs were in the best possible position for punching. To finish off the armaments, he wrapped a heavy steel chain carefully around the top of the gauntlet and looped the end around his wrist.

That took care of the exterior offensives. With his left hand, Chopper filled a small plastic medicine phial from his top pocket. The container had once held harmless saccharine tablets; now the contents were far more powerful and deadly - amphetamine pills.

Even an Angel sometimes lacked that little extra bit of courage or bravado - needed a boost to his already powerful destructive urges. The pep pills always gave that little extra...with a large dose surging power into the body and releasing the conscience mechanism of the brain, an Angel could hurt, even kill, without compunction.

Shaking three of the pills into his hand, Chopper threw back his head to help them down his gullet. The buzz of power from the drug would take about ten minutes to build up in   his body.

Now Chopper was ready for whatever was happening at the scene of the rev-up. He remounted the bike, kicked the engine into life and took away from the pavement with a roar of power and a squeal of rubber on tarmac.

Rounding the corner near the Greek's, Chopper could see that it was a fight. A big one, from the look of things.

About fifteen Angels were scrapping with about half a dozen young Skinheads.

Chopper smiled savagely. The odds were good...fifteen to six. It all helped to nurture and foster the power image. An Angel didn't like to lose a fight.

The Skinheads were probably from the Dalston area, thought Chopper. This fight had been brewing for weeks, ever since an Angel raiding party had descended on a late-night horror film show in the area about a month previously. During the interval, more than twenty of the local youths had discovered cigarette holes burned into their trendy and expensive boutique clothes. Young girls, too, had not escaped. The backs of their dresses bore the marks of black motor oil and the scars of razor-blade cuts.

Passing from seat to seat with lighted cigarettes, burning holes in clothing was a popular Angel pastime for cinemas. Watching the film was for citizens. Destruction was much more fun and in the Angel tradition.

It was highly likely that the Skinheads had come over to the Holloway area in the hopes of finding a few Angel bikes to smash up. One useful form of retaliation was to tip bags of quick-setting cement into petrol tanks or to pour a few cans of paint stripper over the carefully polished bodywork of the machines.

This time, however, the Skinheads were not going to get their revenge. It seemed that they had been interrupted before they could set about their destructive work.

Chopper parked his bike against a wall carefully, and with deliberate and exaggerated slowness. Being cool - and being clearly seen to be cool - was very important. It showed class.

He pulled back the throttle and jammed it in position at about half revs. The gutsy roar of the big Triumph Bonneville added several hundred more decibels to the general racket.

Chopper swaggered slowly towards the thick of the fight, flexing his fingers and gritting his teeth together. There was a head near his foot. Chopper casually looked down at it with disdain. The head had short, cropped hair.

Chopper pulled back his right foot and swung it forward again in a vicious kick. He grinned with sadistic delight as his heavy boot made contact with the kid's skull. The semi-conscious youth released a shriek of agony and passed out completely.

Passing on, Chopper kept a careful eye open for attacks from the side. Another Skinhead staggered backwards, reeling from a punch in the stomach. Chopper's foot lashed out, catching him behind the knees and robbing him of his balance. The youth fell to the ground as Chopper's boot swung into the bridge of the kid's nose, causing a scream of pain and a small fountain of blood.

On his right-hand side, Chopper saw Danny The Deathlover, one of his Angel compatriots. Danny was holding one Skinhead from behind in a full nelson while two others took turns to rain blows into his lower stomach. Chopper paused for a moment to stand in line behind them. When his turn came, Chopper aimed for the soft flesh below the kid's eyes, viciously twisting his wrist as his fist made contact. The sharp studs of the gauntlet gouged into the Skinhead's flesh, tearing and ripping out small triangular-shaped pieces of skin. The chain wrapped around Chopper's wrist flicked upwards sharply with the movement, opening up a nasty-looking gash above the kid's right eyebrow. Blood trickled down his forehead, ran down the valley of his nose, gathered into thick droplets on his chin and dripped slowly on to his shirt.

Danny the Deathlover let the kid go. He sank, whimpering, to the pavement, barely able to move a muscle against the pain. Chopper joined the others in kicking him in the ribs and stomach until he lay half in and half out of the gutter.

'Right fucking place for 'em too,' murmured Danny as he

turned away to seek another target.

Chopper slapped him on the back.

'Hi Danny. Big M here?'

Danny grinned good-naturedly. 'Ain't seen him,' he replied between gasps for breath. 'Maybe he's in the Greek's. This stupid fucking grope-about ain't worth calling a bundle.'

'Watch out...blade,' shouted a disembodied voice from the thick of the fight. Chopper and Danny whirled round quickly, seeking out the source of danger to a fellow Angel.

It was Freaky. Backed against a fence, he was carefully appraising the movements of a Skinhead who circled him menacingly, a wicked looking Bowie knife held at arm's length. The kid lunged forward, aiming for Freaky's stomach. Freaky twisted just in time and pulled sideways, so that the blade sank harmlessly into the wood of the fence.

The Skinhead didn't get a chance to try a second time.

Chopper and Danny the Deathlover were on him before he had freed his knife. They crossed the few intervening yards in double-quick time as one man. A fellow Angel was in trouble - and that meant instant rescue, with no questions asked.

Chopper raised his right arm and brought the end of the heavy bicycle chain down hard across the back of the kid's neck. Danny's bunched fist rammed solidly into the kid's kidneys before he had a chance to turn round. Chopper swung his right foot hard against the Skinhead's ankles, tripping him to the ground.

Freaky grinned thankfully at his rescuers.

'Thanks fellers,' he said simply. 'I'll do the same for you next time.'

The smile on his face faded as he bent over the fallen Skinhead, grabbed him by the lapels of his jacket and hauled him to his feet. Freaky's knee came up under the kid's groin with the speed of a snake striking. As the Skinhead doubled up with pain, Freaky interlocked his fingers, meshing both hands into a solid club and brought it down with all the strength he could muster across the back of the kid's neck.

As the Skinhead fell, his body performed a half-turn towards Chopper and Danny. It was too good an opportunity to miss. Chopper brought up his knee under the kid's face, and felt the personal satisfaction of hearing the crunch of broken bone from his nose.

The Skinhead went down and stayed down, while blows from boots rained upon his body. He lay groaning and writhing in agony, occasionally spitting out gouts of blood and pieces of broken teeth.

'Don't ever try to pull a blade on an Angel,' snapped Freaky before they left him. 'It just ain't friendly.'

A sudden blast of horns cut above the uproar of the fight and the rev-up. Chopper glanced quickly over to where the bikes were parked.

Tiny, waiting on lookout duty, was waving his arms in the accepted warning signal. A couple of Angel birds were controlling the horns.

The Angels dropped the fight right where it was, releasing those Skinheads still lucky enough to be on their feet to retire to lick their wounds. The signal meant that the fuzz were coming. Everyone scrambled for the bikes. There wasn't any need to discuss plans for flight. Everyone knew exactly where to go.

There wasn't a Hells Angel in sight when the police patrol car rounded the corner with its siren blaring. Only six bruised and bleeding Skinheads - three of whom would spend the next four days of their lives in a hospital bed.

The hangout was always Nick the Greek's cafe - commonly known as 'The Greek's' for short. It was the place to meet, the place to make plans - and the place to run for when there was fuzz trouble in the air.

Nobody quite remembered when it had first become the central meeting place, nor why it should have been chosen. It had just happened that way.

The dirty, dingy cafe was exactly right for the Angels. It was tucked away in a back-street, but easily accessible from at least three major roads. It equally gave access to the same three major roads if anyone wanted to get going anywhere in a hurry.

It was more or less equidistant from East Ham and Tottenham, where the two main chapters of the Angels were centred. It was considered to be a fairly 'safe' area...most marauding gangs of Skinheads and Agroboys knew that the place was an Angel stronghold, and wisely stayed clear.

Most of the plastic-topped tables in the cafe bore carved inscriptions of names, memorable events and even some of the highest recorded scores in the gang-bang stakes. Some of the more boastful Angel Mamas had seen fit to record their sexual excesses for posterity. An ordinary Angel bird only got to be a 'Mama' after making at least a token attempt at the standing gang-bang record and by gaining at least the temporary affection of one particular Angel who undertook to become her protector.

The record still stood at the fantastic score of thirty-one Angels satisfied in less than three hours by the Black Bastard - the affectionate name bestowed on one Caroline Munsen, who had achieved great success from mixing Angelhood inclinations with a natural tendency towards nymphomania. She was remembered by many with mixed feelings of fondness and nostalgia.

Caroline had subsequently left the Angels and had married a young toolmaker from Islington. All those who remembered her agreed that at least one aspect of his married life would be more than satisfactory.

Nick the Greek looked up casually as the Angels sauntered into the cafe. He didn't smile - but then Nick never did.

Nick rarely showed even the faintest trace of emotion. It was highly unlikely that he loved the Angels deeply, yet they had poured back a certain amount of regular revenue into his failing back-street business. The Angels were more than the backbone of Nick's business - they made up all but a tiny part of his entire clientele. By their very nature and by their attitude to anyone else who happened to be around, they had become somewhat exclusive customers.

Chopper glanced carefully around the cafe before the main bulk of the Angels walked in. Five or six Angel birds sat around over cold cups of coffee waiting for a fast ride or a quick screw. An elderly meths alkie sat alone in one corner singing softly to himself and smiling stupidly as his eroded mind conjured up his favourite private dream for him. The Angels tolerated drop-outs of his type as harmless extras. They were sufficiently way out of tune with the rest of humanity not to be classed as citizens. The alkies, in turn, tolerated the Angels as another part of the human debris left behind by an ailing society. Or perhaps they didn't even see them through the meths madness.

Of Marty, there was no sign. The fact registered grimly in Chopper's mind.

Marty Gresham, usually known by his Angel name of 'Big M', was acknowledged leader of the group. The distinction was his only because he possessed what was every Angel's dream - a Harley-Davidson motorcycle. A Harley - suitably stripped down and re-modelled - was the ultimate in class. But even with this one outstanding advantage, Big M had fought his way to the leadership and still fought to protect it. He could out-fight, out-ride and out-think any Angel when called upon to do so.

Only lately, Chopper reflected, he hadn't been doing too much of anything.

In Marty's absence, Chopper took control. As officially-appointed Angel lieutenant, he was second-in-command and authorised to organise any activities short of a full-scale run.

Right now, Chopper needed to organise alibis and protection for the gang. It wouldn't be long before the fuzz came round asking certain leading questions about grievous bodily harm to six Skinheads.

Chopper nodded towards Nick, who shrugged his expansive shoulders almost imperceptibly by way of recognition.

'Nick, some of the boys would like to wash up,' said Chopper.

Nick nodded understanding, and gestured to the door behind

the serving counter.

'OK fellers...anyone with traces of blood on their hands go out back and wash up,' snapped Chopper.

Several of the Angels filed past Chopper and Nick in orderly fashion and disappeared into the kitchen.

Chopper looked down at his own hands. They were clean. He had taken the precaution of wiping off the blood on a fallen Skinhead's shirt before leaving the scene of the fight.

He ran a rough count of numbers, including spare birds sitting around the place.

'Eighteen coffees, Nick,' he said.

Nick the Greek busied himself with the Italian expresso machine, which spluttered and hissed fiercely. Nick lined the coffees on the counter and as the Angels filed out of the kitchen, they picked them up one by one as though they were soldiers going through the mess hall.

Chopper picked up a couple of spare cups and carried them over to the girls.

'OK Doreen,' he said to one of them with a smile. 'You know the routine. When the fuzz ask questions, we've all been in here for at least an hour.'

'Tell 'em yourself, Chopper,' replied Doreen, nodding her head towards the door of the cafe over Chopper's shoulder. He turned round. Two uniformed policemen were just coming in.

Nick's face was expressionless.

'What can I do for you gentlemen?' he asked without a trace of sarcasm. There was just a trace of injured pride and wonderment in his voice - as though he had been bitterly hurt to unjustly deserve a visit from the custodians of law and order.

'Crowded tonight Nick,' said one of the policemen pointedly. 'Had a sudden influx of business have you?'

Nick shrugged. 'You know this business,' he said. 'They come in, buy one cup of coffee and stay for hours. Been like that all night.'

'Sure, Nick,' agreed the second copper, the disbelief obvious in his voice. 'We wouldn't want to pull you in as an accessory after the fact, would we, Nick?'

Nick's face showed no trace of animation. He turned away and busied himself wiping up cups with a grey, greasy dishcloth.

'I just try to run my business and mind my own business,' he said blankly.

The faintest trace of exasperation could be seen on the second policeman's face.

'One of these days your business is going to be ours, Nick,' he said menacingly. 'Tonight it could nearly have been murder.'

Chopper stood up and walked over to the coppers. He could see a golden opportunity to show some real class by a bit of fuzz-baiting.

'Been an accident has there, officer?' he asked in an innocent voice. Repressed laughter bubbled out and rippled around the cafe as the other Angels saw the inherent humour in the conversation.

The cop's mouth tightened into a grim line. He knew the only way to deal with an Angel was to return sarcasm with sarcasm. Nothing hurt an Angel more than to be belittled in front of his mates.

'Well if it isn't Adolph Hitler's daughter herself,' said the copper. 'Come to ask for directions somewhere have you love?'

Chopper instantly regretted his move. He hadn't expected the policeman to counter in this way. He struggled quickly to think of a suitably crushing answer to save face.

'Yeah - I wondered if you could tell me where the local policeman's ball is being held,' he said quickly. 'I feel very strongly about supporting policemen's balls...they probably need it.'

The line worked. Another ripple of laughter went round the cafe. The cop smiled indulgently.

'Funny little fellow,' he murmured to his companion. 'I think we ought to see his licence, don't you?' He turned his attention to Chopper once more.

'I take it you do have a scooter or something?' he asked. 'We'd like to see your licence...just to find out whether you've passed the driving test or not.'

Chopper realised he was caught in a trap of his own making. If he meekly produced his licence, he would have been shown up in front of the gang. If he argued, the fuzz were likely to turn nasty and search him...and he was still holding the amphetamine pills. It was a nasty situation.

Danny the Deathlover came to his rescue.

'Hey, fellers...the fuzz want to see our licences,' he shouted. The other Angels got the message. Chopper - and therefore everything the Angels stood for - was being held up to ridicule by the cops. Something had to be done to restore the rightful balance.

Everyone got up and walked across to the two policemen. 'I got a dog licence,' shouted Danny the Deathlover.

'My old man renewed his TV licence last week,' put in Freaky.

'Do we need a licence to fuck policemen's daughters?' called out another voice, carefully hidden in the crowd.

'Hey, Nick...show him your food vendor's licence,' called out Chopper, warming to the new twist in the game.

Doreen came over. 'I got a green card from the VD ward...will that do?' she asked. A guffaw of laughter greeted this latest offering.

'So you're the bitch who knocked us all up,' said Screwball Sam with good-natured humour. Another great roar of laughter.

'Yeah - that's what comes of dating police cadets,' retorted Doreen quickly. 'I only did it out of pity, and look what I get for my trouble.'

The policemen were surrounded by the jeering Angels. Backed up against the serving counter, they could only face the barrage of jokes and abuse or push their way though to the door.

They chose the latter course. There was nothing to be gained from prolonging the situation now that they had lost the advantage.

'Mind how you drive,' said Chopper as they climbed into the Panda car. 'The police round here are pretty sharp.'

As the police car drove off, the Angels filtered back into the cafe, still laughing and joking amongst themselves about the situation.

Danny sidled up to Chopper.

'Hey, man - you really let those pigs fuck you up,' he said reproachfully.

Chopper tried not to let Danny see how rattled he was.

'Bastards,' he spat viciously. 'They were just trying to be smart.'

Danny wasn't convinced.

Chopper's control snapped.

'Yeah - but Marty ain't here, is he?' he accused. 'Same as he ain't been here for the last two bundles. Seems to me that Marty isn't doing too much of anything lately - except telling everyone what he would have done if he'd been somewhere he wasn't.'

Danny the Deathlover's eyes widened in surprise. It wasn't like Chopper to criticise Big M. Chopper was usually a pretty righteous Angel - respecting the Angel code and showing nothing but respect and admiration for the acknowledged leader.

Danny felt that he had to put in a word for Big M in his absence.

'I guess he's been busy or something, huh?' he said.

Chopper saw the offered way out and took it. Saving face was of vital importance always.

'Yeah. I guess he has,' he agreed. 'Still...we really showed those bastards up, didn't we?'

'You bet we did,' said Danny, and grinned widely. The tension dropped out of the air. Normal balance was restored. The Angels were united and had come out on top against a common enemy. Things were exactly as they should be.

❝ What we gonna do, then?' asked Danny.

Chopper looked once more round the assembled personages in the Greek's and shrugged his shoulders apathetically. 'Any ideas?' he ventured, feeling that anything he could suggest would be an anti-climax anyway to the brief fuzz raid.

'That's your department,' Danny pointed out. Chopper saw the veiled rebuke and decided not to acknowledge it.

Chopper grinned amiably.

'The Angels are a democratic constitution,' he murmured. Anything approaching a deep or vaguely intellectual statement usually reduced Danny the Deathlover to zero status. Danny grinned stupidly and shrugged his shoulders.

'Well, if there ain't going to be anything organised,' he said slowly, 'I was thinking of pulling Doreen for a screw...that is, unless you want to give it a pull.'

'No - help yourself,' Chopper offered generously. The two might just as well have been discussing who handed out the cigarettes. Angel sheep of Doreen's status were communal property.

'Are you sure?' asked Danny.

'Sure.'

Danny fidgeted nervously, still not sure whether he was keeping in line by cutting out with Doreen.

'OK - then I'll cut out then,' he said at last.

'Yeah. Give a couple of thumps for me, Man,' said Chopper as Danny walked over towards where Doreen sat with her mate. Danny mumbled something in her ear. Doreen smiled, nodded her head and stood up. The two of them strolled out of the Greek's without a backward glance and Chopper heard the sound of Danny's stripped-down Velocette starting up.

The bike roared off, the sound seeming to hand behind in the air like a cloud of exhaust fumes for a few seconds.

Chopper checked around once more for signs of action. Max and Freaky were indulging in an arm-wrestling contest on one of the tables, whilst Screwball Sam and Irish Mick held burning gas lighters under their wrists. Doreen's spotty blonde friend had moved over to chat up Duke, and two other Angels had bought packets of peanuts and were throwing them at the alkie in the corner. The idea of the game seemed to be to land one of the nuts in either his half-open mouth or in his cup of long-cold tea. Chopper smiled good naturedly at this little charade. It was nice of the boys to include an outsider in Angel sport.

The night was dead. The fuzz had seen to that. There seemed nothing for it but to cut out and maybe take in a few beers on the way home.

Suddenly Chopper wished he had exercised his rights as lieutenant to help himself to Doreen. A screw would have been better than nothing, he reflected. Still, he reminded himself, picking up one of the sheep wouldn't have showed very good class in front of the rest. Just lately, Chopper had been relying too heavily on ordinary Angel chicks for his sex kicks. Nobody had actually said anything directly, although Big M had pointed out a couple of times that a second-in-command really ought to have a regular Mama of his own.

Chopper smiled grimly to himself at the thought. It was all right for Marty to talk - he had Elaine. Having a Mama was just great when she was blonde, beautiful, young and as full of fire as a volcano. A woman like that was worth holding on to, worth raising to the status of Mama and even admitting grudging respect to.

The sheep were just for quick sexual release...like a flash was for bringing up stale beer and vomit and a crash was for tired Angels who had just taken part in a heavy fight. As far as Chopper was concerned, a screw was a screw was a screw - but worrying about it too much was a hassle.

The thought of Elaine brought a quick surge of envy with it...or was the feeling simply that? Chopper checked his thoughts quickly, knowing that his inner mind was getting out of line again. He'd been doing it far too much lately - criticising Big M, nagging himself because he couldn't afford a Harley-D, feeling that the Angels were being watered-down from their original outrageous aims.

Chopper hammered home facts and rules of conduct into his brain like a doubting cleric reminds himself of his slipping religious convictions. He was a Hells Angel - and a righteous one at that. To say righteous, he had to stay with the code, abide by the rules and follow the doctrines rigidly. He was number two in line - and until Big M relinquished command, or got killed, that was what he would stay.

Still...the nagging doubts persisted in his mind. Where was Marty these days? Was he slipping away from the Angels? Were they all suffering from a growing weakness because their leader had ceased to command as forcefully? Was Big M's time as leader about through?...And what, if anything, to do about it?

A mental picture of Elaine's waist-length blonde hair and flashing blue eyes popped up in his mind for a split second before Chopper finally cleared his brain and returned to the reality of the present. She was sitting astride a black and white Harley-Davidson motor-cycle, with chromium-plated twin tanks and extended front forks. She was smiling at him, a strange, half-promising, half-mocking smile.

His mind was made up. Chopper picked up his keys from the table and stood up to leave.

'See you guys,' he shouted to everyone in general. 'Going to get me some private action.'

A chorus of whistles and signals of approval answered him as he headed out of the Greek's. It was good class to suggest that he was going to something other than the clapped-out atmosphere of the Greek's. It was certainly better than admitting he would probably spend a couple of hours drinking lonesome pints of bitter and a couple more sitting in his mall bedsitter, playing old Jerry Lee Lewis records to himself.

Chopper kicked over the Triumph, taking care not to rev up as he cruised off. Revving up and taking away with a squeal of tyres was considered very uncool in the presence of other Angels. That routine was used merely to annoy citizens and to demonstrate bravado in front of the fuzz. His arms draped limply over the ape-hanger handlebars, Chopper executed a double circle in front of the Greek's by way of statutory salute and eased off down the side streets.

He headed for Hackney, debating with himself where to go for a drink. It had to be somewhere 'safe' now that he was on his own. Any pair of Skinheads would consider themselves the luckiest kids in town to lay hands on an unprotected Angel lieutenant.

As he cruised along. Chopper decided to skip the drink and

take a bit of a run instead. Perhaps a really decent burst of speed could clear out the cloudy thoughts in his head tonight. He headed for the Stratford flyover on the A1.

The flyover had been a good idea, thought Chopper as he came up to the approach. It was something of a symbol to all the Angels in his chapter, since Little Willie had snuffed out there only eight months previously.

Once over the approach ramp, there was about five hundred yards before the apex of the flyover, which curved very gently to the left. The five hundred yards gave one a chance to accelerate to top speed, so that you hit the top and with luck took both wheels off the ground. The trick was bringing both wheels on to the road surface once more in perfect alignment, yet still being ready to take the slight bend. At speeds of over ninety miles an hour, it was a difficult and dangerous game to play...as Little Willie had found.

Willie had let his front wheel twist slightly while the bike was temporarily airborne. On making contact with the road again, the extended front forks of his bike had snatched at the sudden friction, wresting the handlebars from his grasp. The bike had slewed across the road, hit the crash-barrier and stopped dead. Willie hadn't. His body had plummeted down to the road forty feet below.

Just in case that hadn't been enough to take him out of this life with full Angel honours, a passing petrol tanker had rumbled over his prone body, smashing his spine in three places.

Only Danny the Deathlover had been with Little Willie when the accident had occurred.

His only comment had been: 'Man, when I snuff I want it to be as beautiful and as glorious as that was.'

The night Little Willie had died was also the night that Danny Reardon had been given his Angel nickname.

Chopper came up to the flyover with a healthy respect for the dangers ahead of him. He didn't share Danny's death wish, and had no intention of sharing Little Willie's fate.

...But the flyover was a symbol of everything which was best about the Angels. It represented their guts, their contempt for danger and their sheer skill in handling a powerful hog. It also represented the constant need to prove themselves to themselves, the desire to reassure themselves that they were Angels, and no common breed of pig citizen.

Chopper throttled up savagely, feeling the machine between his legs surge forward angrily. Just before the top of the flyover, he allowed his eyes to stray from the road for just long enough to check the speedometer. It registered ninety-seven miles per hour. Chopper was grinning savagely as the bike mounted the slight hump and soared two feet clear of the ground below. For something like five-eighths of a second, Chopper and his hog were flying, free of the ground and free from the world.

The front tyre screamed in agony as rubber bit into tarmac once again and the shock bypassed the absorbers to vibrate up through the forks, into the handlebars and along Chopper's arms. He was down and safe. He slipped the throttle back gently and the bike ground back into the seventies.

He slowed to fifty as he came up to the roundabout, finally taking the curve round at a sedate forty-five. He was still grinning, pleased that he had broken his own exiting record for the flyover. It had been a good run - his previous best speed smashed by a clear two miles an hour and only one below Big M's accredited speed of ninety-eight. One of these days, Chopper told himself, he was going to make Big M's record look like that of a scooter on a steep hill...but to do that he needed the extra weight and the extra power of the Harley-D.

Feeling highly satisfied with himself, Chopper brought the Triumph lazily round the roundabout with his right footrest only a few inches from the ground, straightened up and headed homewards at a comfortable cruising speed.

He didn't need a drink any more and there wasn't the slightest desire for sex in his head. Speed was an incredibly sensual thrill in itself, a substitute for sex which was more exhilarating than the real thing. The sense of achievement he had gained from the flyover run was as electrifying as any orgasm could possibly be.

The night was salvaged. It had been a good trip and his head was cleared of all the shit which had been filling it up. Chopper Harris felt good, glad to be alive and glad to be a Hells Angel.

Chopper parked the bike at the side of the kerb and locked the front wheels. In the absence of a garage to hide it, some sort of security precautions were necessary. The Triumph was so obviously an Angel bike - bearing its 'One Percenter' motif proudly - that it would be a prime target for any passing gangs of Skinheads. Chopper always left it in a quiet back street behind the flatlet house he lived in, but he still had constant nightmares about finding it battered and mutilated with paint stripper, or of losing it altogether. Quite apart from the Skinhead danger, there was always the possibility that a couple of young Greasers might happen by it, decide to elevate themselves from leather-jacketed street-walkers and play at being Hells Angels for the night.

He patted the machine lovingly on the handlebars as he left it. It was a gesture of true affection for the thing he loved and respected most in life.

Chopper walked round the house to the front entrance, fishing in his pocket for his front-door key as he went. As he came near the front of the house he saw that he had visitors.

Gleaming proudly under the yellow glare of the street lamp stood Marty's Harley-D. Of Big M himself, there was no sign. Chopper looked around carefully, shrugged and walked up the short drive to the house.

'Hi, Man,' said Marty's voice as he reached the porch.

Chopper glanced down. Marty sat in the shadows of the concealed porch, lounging with his back against the wall and both legs dangling over the top step. Beside him, head resting between his thighs, was Elaine.

'Where you been, Man?' drawled Big M casually. 'We dropped in at the Greek's and Freaky said you cut out. Been waiting an hour, Man.'

'Went for a run,' replied Chopper as casually as possible. He didn't want to mention the flyover incident. That was his - private.

'Coming in?' he asked as he placed his key in the lock of the door.

'Yeah we'll come in for a while,' said Marty. 'Got a little bit of shit left if you fancy a smoke.'

'Can't be bad,' said Chopper coolly. 'I got some leaves

upstairs.'

He opened the door, pushing it aside to let Elaine and Marty in before him. Protocol was established.

The three climbed the four flights of stairs to the top landing. Chopper unlocked the door of his room and showed them in. He snapped on the light and sprawled on the floor. Marty took the one chair and Elaine curled at his feet like a dog.

'Want a beer?' asked Chopper after a few silent seconds.

'Yeah. Why not?'

Chopper stood up, crossed the small room to the kitchenette and pulled a quart bottle of light ale from the food cabinet. Opening it, he carried it across to Marty.

Marty put the bottle to his lips and took a long, deep swill of luke-warm beer. Passing the bottle down to Elaine, he lounged back in the chair as she sipped at it.

'So where you been?' Marty repeated.

Chopper realised that he wasn't going to get away with secrecy.

'Made a crack at the flyover,' he admitted grudgingly.

Big M nodded knowingly. 'What'd you make?'

'Ninety-seven.'

Marty's eyebrows raised very slightly. He sucked at his teeth and shook his head in a gesture of acceptance.

'Not bad. You're coming up on me, Chopper.'

Elaine spoke for the first time.

'Still number two, eh, Chopper?' she said mockingly. 'You're gonna have to try harder.' She and Marty glanced at each other and smiled at the shared joke. Chopper forced himself to grin good-naturedly.

'You could always lend me your hog so a real record could be set,' joked Chopper in return. This was good for a grin all round - no Angel leader yet had lent his bike to a living soul.

'Yeah - I'll lend you the hog when I lend you Ellie,' said Marty with a smile which revealed all of his possessiveness and the certainty of his control. As if to illustrate his point he reached down, sliding his arm round Elaine's waist and handling her left breast lovingly. Elaine looked up and smiled as Marty fondled her breast. Turning slightly, she nuzzled into his lap and planted a kiss upon the zipper of his denim jeans.

'Later baby, later,' said Marty teasingly.

Chopper laughed nervously. Seeing the obvious sexuality in Elaine hit him with the force of a lightning bolt somewhere deep inside the groin. A mental picture of Elaine's naked body flashed across his brain. In a secondary day dream, he pictured his own nude body sprawled across hers, his hands clasped around those full, magnificent breasts and his lips clamped firmly on those full, red soft lips of hers. Within the space of a split second, Chopper cajoled, teased, excited and finally fulfilled her. Elaine's orgasm crashed against him, the hot gush of her orgasm bathed his thighs and trickled wetly down his legs.

Chopper stood up quickly, the action serving to cut short the erotic dream and return him to reality.

The room...his room...the people in it - all part and parcel of the rigid system he accepted because he must accept. There was a reality and there were dreams. The two were distinctly separate because they had to be separate. There could be no bridge between the two worlds of dreams and reality.

Elaine was Big M's girl. Big M was his superior. Elaine was as exclusively Marty's as his leadership position was. No-one changed the way things were. No-one in his right mind even attempted to dream them any differently.

'How about this smoke,' Chopper blurted out. 'I'll go get some leaves.'

He ran from the danger across the reality of his bedsitting room, over to the reality of his chest of drawers, searching out the reality of a packet of cigarette papers.

Hashish, the magical substance which would fill those cigarette papers was the stuff of dreams. Not thoughts about real people, in a real situation.

Drug hallucinations were viable, acceptable alternatives to reality. You didn't attempt to remodel or change what was real by positive action. You smoked pot and accepted a negative escape route which led into other avenues of a changed status quo.

Chopper's fingers were trembling as he rummaged through the drawer, turning over socks and handkerchiefs and packets of contraceptives searching for the small packet of liquorice cigarette papers. Finding them, he fought for control of his own impulses for several seconds before returning.

'Here you are, Marty. You want to do the honours?'

The question was irrelevant, pointless and answered before asked. Of course Marty would roll the joints - that was his prerogative - both as supplier of the drug and as his superior status decreed.

Marty accepted the papers and laid them down upon the floor in front of him. Pulling a twenty pack of cigarettes from his pocket, he pulled out a long sliver of the silver paper and deftly removed the tissue paper from one side of it.

He delved into another pocket, pulling out a small, nut-sized piece of silver foil. He unwrapped it carefully, exposing the tiny piece of chocolate-coloured drug inside. Breaking off a piece, he wrapped it carefully in the silver paper from the cigarette packet, twisting it into a tiny ball.

Chopper and Elaine sat silently on the floor as Marty went through the ritualistic preparation of the pot. Holding the tiny silver ball gently between finger and thumb, Marty flicked his cigarette and cooked the raw hashish by flame. When the faintest aroma of burning hash reached his nostrils, Marty placed the hot silver paper on the floor and reached for the packet of cigarette papers. Extracting three, he overlaid them to form the pattern for the joint, crumbled a cigarette between his fingers and laid the tobacco in a slim tube along the papers.

The hash went in, finely crumbled between finger and thumb and with every last grain carefully brushed off the fingers and into the joint. A small piece of tissue paper crumpled up to serve as a filter completed the preparation. Big M picked up the papers carefully and gently, and with well-practised fingers rolled them into a long cylindrical shape.

He held the joint downwards for Elaine to lick along the edge and nodding to signify that the operation was complete. Marty dextrously rolled the joint between his fingers, pressing every part of the edges together so that the joint held firmly.

The reefer was ready. Marty rolled it gently along the palm of one hand to tighten up the mixture of tobacco and hashish. He raised it to his lips, cigarette lighter at the ready.

'Just a sec,' said Elaine suddenly, pulling on Marty's wrist and pulling the joint clear from his mouth. 'The scene doesn't look so good to me.' She nodded towards Chopper meaningfully.

'How do you mean, babe?' asked Marty.

Elaine smiled wickedly.

'Well you know how randy I get on that stuff,' she said. 'Maybe we ought to pull in a spare bird or something, in case it hits Chopper the same way.'

Marty smiled and turned to Chopper.

'Good idea?' he asked.

Once again, Chopper faced the tension of the situation and his brain raced as he tried to think how best to play cool.

Elaine was a bitch, he reflected bitterly. She had deliberately engineered the situation, knowing what a spot it would put him in. She was, in fact, making an obvious point of the fact that Chopper had no Mama to rely upon. She was taking the chance of making him feel small, reminding him of the fact that she was Big M's girl and that she knew how much Chopper fancied her. She was making him sweat and she knew it.

There was only one thing to do; keep cool and show class by refusing to be hassled. Chopper took it as the only way out.

'OK - procure for me,' he said. He stared Elaine levelly in the eyes. They were dancing mischievously, and no-one could have missed the wicked glint of triumph which crossed them.

'Where's the phone?' she asked standing up.

'In the hall downstairs,' said Chopper, gesturing towards the door.

'I'll go phone Samantha,' said Elaine, and disappeared outside.

Chopper fumed quietly. Blast the girl, she knew exactly how and where to strike so as to hurt most...And she always did it when she, Chopper and Marty were together.

'That chick of yours sure likes riding me,' Chopper complained.

'Yeah - I'd noticed,' agreed Marty with a wry grin. 'If I didn't know better I'd say she fancies you.'

The words caught Chopper in the throat and he caught his breath. He glanced for a split second into Marty's eyes. They wore not even the faintest trace of a smile. He was almost serious...almost because he was saying something his own ego wouldn't let him fully believe.

Suddenly, Chopper saw the answer to many of the things

which had been puzzling him. Now it all made sense - the way Elaine was always making jibes at him, taunting him, trying to force comparisons between him and Big M. She really did fancy him...Big M was only holding on to her by a slim thread. The big fire had gone out and Elaine was looking for new fuel to burn.

...And at the same time, Chopper realised clearly for the first time that it was exactly what he wanted. He wanted to take Elaine all right - but not just because she was Marty's...she was the symbol of Big M's leadership as much as his hog was...And Chopper wanted to take over that leadership. The first lieutenant wanted to snatch the promotion which could never be his any other way.

Chopper forced himself to laugh heartily.

'I should be so bloody lucky,' he said, and noticed with relief that a smile returned to Marty's eyes.

Now he knew something else as well, and the thought sank into his brain as extra ammunition for whenever he should need it. Big M was scared...frightened of losing his control because he could already see that he was losing out. Maybe he was going soft - losing his Angel convictions in the face of a more powerful urge.

Chopper knew that Marty loved Elaine a lot more than he cared to admit. He was obsessed with the girl, and despite his bravado and outward appearance of being cool, he was like putty in her hands.

Chopper's lips curled in an involuntary sneer. Perhaps Marty even had visions of marriage, semi-detached houses, nappies and flying ducks upon the wall. Maybe he wanted to exchange the smell of exhaust fumes for the stink of urine-soaked nappies, and swap his Angel colours for a pin-stripe suit and a bowler.

Everything suddenly came together in Chopper's head. Now he knew exactly what he wanted and he had a rough idea of how he was going to get it.

'I guess you heard about the action tonight,' he said casually.

Big M nodded.

'Yeah - Freaky said you had a bundle with the Dalston boyos.'

'That's right,' said Chopper, 'It was a good scene - you shouldn't have missed it.'

The words were a rebuke - thinly disguised, and Marty didn't miss the underlying meaning.

'Yeah - pity about that. Had other things going for me,' he said defensively. He jerked a thumb towards the half-open door. 'That bird takes a lot of looking after, Man.'

'I bet,' said Chopper and smiled as he knew he was supposed to do. However, he wasn't going to change the subject, even though Marty was making it obvious that he wanted him to. Chopper intended to press home his advantage while he still held it.

'Listen. Marty...are you not happy with the way things are going lately or something?' Chopper enquired.

Marty looked puzzled. 'What do you mean, Man?'

'I mean you've not been around as much as usual just lately, that's all. I wondered if there was anything behind it.'

Marty's eyes narrowed to slits as he recognised the indirect challenge.

'Just what's on your mind, Chopper?'

'The boys are beginning to notice, Marty...they say things, y'know?'

'No I don't know,' snapped Marty. 'What sort of things?'

Chopper fidgeted nervously.

'Well, not to mention any names or anything...I've just sort of heard it mentioned that you might be a bit bugged off with the chapter, that's all.'

'That's crap and you know it Chop.'

'Yeah - but you've got to admit you've not been around too much lately Marty.'

'Look, Man...so I missed out on a rumble tonight and maybe two nights a week I don't get down to the Greek's...so what do you think, I've become a fucking head or something?'

'It ain't me Marty so much as the rest of the guys. You know damn well I've always stuck with you.'

Marty stared calmly into Chopper's eyes without wavering.

'Yeah, so far,' he muttered blankly, and the irony in his voice was obvious.

Chopper decided he had pushed the situation far enough for one night.

'So Marty Gresham is still Big M, eh?' he said.

Marty jabbed his finger angrily towards the colours on his jacket. Just above the Hells Angel symbol of the death's head with tiny wings and a motorcycle helmet was a small strip of red ribbon.

It was the leader's symbol.

'What the hell do you think I wear this for, Chop...some sort of game?'

'OK, Man - forget it,' said Chopper.

'You're lucky it's September, Marty,' said Elaine's voice as she returned. 'If it was anywhere near the ninth of March I'd say you had a problem, Man.'

'What you talking about Ellie?'

'Ides of March, Marty, that's all. Chopper knows all about that crap, don't you, Chopper? Some of that fancy education of his.'

Marty turned to Chopper in bewilderment.

'What the fuck is she rambling about, Chop?'

'It's a joke, Marty. Just a joke about something that happened in Ancient Rome.'

'Jesus...you bloody smart asses have a fucking weird sense of humour,' Marty spat sarcastically.

The subject was dropped, but Chopper caught the amused twinkle in Elaine's eyes.

'Sammy's coming round in about ten minutes,' she announced.

'I'll roll another joint,' said Marty and set about going through the entire ritual again.

Elaine sat down on the floor at his feet and continued to smile mockingly at Chopper.

'You might thank me,' she said simply.

'For what?'

Her face faded and for a second Chopper caught a piercing look which suggested that Elaine was still not quite sure of him.

'Because it never hurts to know where your friends are,' she said pointedly. 'Sometimes you need a little help to get things the way you want them to be.'

There was no need to reply. Chopper raised his eyebrows as a sign that he had understood her meaning. Elaine turned her attention back to Marty.

'Once an Angel, always an Angel,' she murmured to him.

'Isn't that right, Big M?'

'That's right baby,' said Marty, running his fingers through her mane of blonde hair. 'You hold on to what you got.'

'Sure - for as long as you can,' added Elaine, but Marty failed to see the significance of the remark.

Marty continued rolling the second joint. There was silence for a couple of minutes. Finally Marty spoke again.

'Listen, Chop - it's about time I planned a run or something, eh?'

'Yeah. It might be a good idea, Big M. The boys are a bit restless for some action.'

Marty nodded. 'That's what I thought. How about hitting Dalston again as a reprisal for that bundle tonight?'

Elaine spoke up. 'Marty, why not organise something we can all go out on?' she asked. 'The trouble with going for bundles is that all the chicks have to screw around waiting in the Greek's for hours on end. What say we hit somewhere this weekend?'

'What you got in mind, babe?' asked Marty.

Elaine shrugged. 'Anywhere, I guess...thought it might be nice to go down to the coast - hit one of the holiday towns.'

Marty digested this for a while.

'What do you think, Chopper?'

'Sounds good.'

'OK, Man. Roust up the boys tomorrow...that gives 'em two days to get everything ready for Saturday. We'll go down in the morning, about ten.'

'Where?' Elaine wanted to know.

'Oh, I don't know...Southend, Bournemouth maybe...any-where. I'll think about it.'

The bell above Chopper's door buzzed gently, cutting off any further discussion.

'That'll be Sammy,' said Elaine, scrambling to her feet. 'I'll go down and let her in.'

'Yeah - it'll be nice taking the chicks out for a run,' murmured Marty as she left the room.

'It's been quite a time,' said Chopper, remembering that the chapter hadn't taken a full-scale run for something like four months.

Marty didn't answer.

'OK...where's the action then?' It was Samantha, bubbling

and excited as usual, probably because she was stuffed up to the eyeballs already with amphetamines.

'Hiya Chopper. Elaine says you got something good for me.'

'Yeah - me, baby.'

Sammy laughed. 'That's good enough. Plenty of it and bit of variety...that's what keeps a girl going.'

'Come and squat, Sammy,' said Marty patting the floor. 'We're all ready to light up.'

Samantha sank to the floor on Marty's left-hand side. Elaine sat on his right and Chopper crouched down facing the three of them. Marty lit the joint and inhaled the first drag deeply, holding it in his lungs for a few seconds before passing it to Elaine.

The joint passed slowly round the quartet, imparting its magical qualities slowly but surely.

Time started to slow down to take account of this alteration in the state of reality. The worlds of actuality and fantasy prepared themselves for a merger. The room filled with the acrid fumes of burning hashish.

No-one spoke for several minutes as the first joint burned away to a tiny stub. Sucking a last, desperate drag from it, Chopper crushed it into an ashtray and looked hopefully towards Marty. He was already lighting up the second one.

'Hey - this is good shit,' said Samantha suddenly, breaking the bond of silence for the first time.

'You're getting a buzz, eh?' asked Elaine, her voice slightly thickened and slurred by the early effect of the drug.

'Yes...I'm just about ready to go for a flight,' said Samantha and giggled insanely. She leaned over and pressed herself against Chopper. 'You coming with me?'

'Sure baby,' Chopper muttered. 'Just let me catch up with where the world's going.'

Elaine shivered nervously. Chopper looked at her face and felt a sudden wave of desire for her. Elaine's mouth was   half-open, and her breathing was already deeper and more irregular. From time to time, her tongue sneaked out and ran slowly and sensuously across her top lip. Her eyes rolled gently as if in the throes of sexual orgasm.

His eyes fell to her breasts, heaving gently beneath the thin sweater she wore. Chopper wanted to reach out, take both soft, full globes in his hands and crush them until they burst open like over-ripe melons.

He was suddenly aware of a hand in his lap, slowly stroking the insides of his thighs and cupping underneath his groin, squeezing and exploring gently. Dreamily, he tore his eyes away from Elaine to look at the hand, tracing it slowly back along a slim arm to Samantha, who stared at him with wide-eyed wonderment. She, too, was becoming rapidly aroused. Her lips were parted, her eyes heavy and glazed with passion, and between gasps for breath, small moaning sounds escaped from her mouth.

Chopper leaned over and planted a kiss upon her ripe lips, gently at first but quickly responding to her passion as her hot tongue forced itself past his teeth to whip around the insides of his lips and mouth like a wild snake.

He raised his hand to her neck, tracing a line from her throat, down through the soft hollows in her neck and into the recesses of her cleavage hidden by a multi-coloured blouse. His fingers picked impatiently at the buttons, revealing more and more of her breasts held firmly inside a blue flowered brassiere. Chopper probed inside the cups of the bra, forcing back the soft elastic of the material so that his fingertips could trace the soft roundness of them. One finger brushed momentarily across an erected nipple and Samantha shuddered at the stimulus. Her hand, still roving around his lap, moved upwards to catch on his zipper. Gripping the top of the zip fastener between finger and thumb, she began to tug at it feverishly, trying to pull the zip past the obstruction of his throbbing erection.

Elaine stood up, suddenly and with the light of devilment burning in her eyes. With one deft movement, she peeled the sweater up her back and over her head. She cast the sweater to the floor and reached behind her back to unclip her bra. As the garment fell to the floor, her magnificent rounded breasts swung freely.

Samantha was forgotten. Chopper's hand fell from her breasts and he was no longer even aware that she was pulling at the waistband of his jeans, trying to slip them down across his hips. His eyes were on Elaine - as she so obviously wanted them to be.

For she was stripping for him, not for Marty. She had her back to Marty, she had shown her contempt by ignoring him. He lay back half-prone on the floor, the reefer still dangling from his slack lips. Marty's dreams were somewhere else, on a plane of existence which did not fully recognise the sexuality all around him.

Chopper stared, unable to move his eyes away as Elaine fiddled with her skirt. Freed, the garment slid down her nylon-clad legs with a soft rustling sound to lie in a crumpled heap by her feet. She stepped out of the skirt casually, shaking her body gently so that her breasts quivered like soft blancmanges.

She wore no slip...only a pair of tights pulled up over a pair of blue panties which matched the brassiere. Hooking her thumbs into the waistband of the tights, she tugged at them gently, softly moving her body in a swaying motion all the time.

The tights were rolled down to the level of her panties now.

Chopper still stared, unable to fully comprehend, but dimly aware that this entire show was for his benefit.

There was no Samantha, no Big M, no status and rank and no codes to be observed. There was just him, and Elaine...a man and a beautiful woman and they were alone and thrilling to each other's bodies.

The panties started to come down with the tights. Chopper saw the first wisps of curly, fair hair appearing over the top...So she really was a natural blonde, his mind rambled. She really was as perfect as he had so often dreamed she must be.

Samantha was not giving up. Her female ego wouldn't let her admit that another woman's body could cheat her from getting what she wanted so desperately. With a vicious wrench, she pulled the tight hipster jeans free and started to slip them down Chopper's legs.

He wasn't even aware of her attentions as Elaine stood in front of him, beautifully naked. The wicked, mocking smile played on her moist lips. Her eyes held only promise...and a challenge to him.

Marty stirred on the floor as though awakening from his dream and finally realising what was going on.

Weakly, he reached upwards to grab Elaine as though to pull her to him and re-establish his rights to her, but it was not really necessary.

The show was already over. Elaine had turned from Chopper and was about to sink back onto the floor with her man.

She had shown Chopper what was his if and when he wanted

to take it. She had made her play, teased him as far as she was willing to at the moment. Now she was showing him that she was unattainable as long as things stayed the way they were. Changes had to be made - and she was willing to go the way of change herself.

All these things ran through Chopper's befuddled mind as he felt Samantha's warm lips press down on to the soft flesh of his belly. Her wet tongue probed down the line of his thighs as her hands sought to peel off his jacket and rip at the buttons of his shirt.

Visions of Elaine crumbled slowly from his mind as the immediateness of Samantha's sexual fervour got through to him. Almost despite himself, Chopper felt the old routine cycle of his strong sexual urges take control of him.

Like a robot responding to pre-arranged signal commands, he pulled Samantha's body to his and performed the functions expected of him.

As they fell to the floor, Chopper caught a glimpse of Elaine and Marty from the corner of his eye. She had abandoned herself to him like a wild animal, her long red nails clawing at him and digging into the flesh of his back.

Samantha pulled at him, forcing him down upon her.

'Fuck me, for Christ sake fuck me,' she whispered hoarsely in his ear.

The full force of the drug hit Chopper as he fell across her, abandoning himself to the immediate pleasures of copulation.

A scream of pleasure escaped from Elaine's lips at the very second he reached his orgasm.

Chopper smiled grimly. It was somehow strangely prophetic and poetic.

The days to the weekend seemed to drag. Time always passed slowly when there was something to look forward to.

For the next two days, Chopper busied himself rounding up Angels who hadn't been around for a while and making sure his hog was in top notch order.

Of Marty, there was no sign. Not that it was unusual, having given word for the run. Chopper, as lieutenant, was expected to do the actual organisation and preparation.

On Friday night, Chopper rode down to the Greek's. The small cafe was filled to bursting point. It was like a convention.

Chopper grinned happily as he walked in to a chorus of welcomes and good wishes. Looking around, he picked out riders and friends he hadn't seen in months, and many new faces from other chapters.

It would be a really good run, he thought as he counted denim jackets. At least 45 Angels, plus up to 30 chicks.

The usual complement of Greasers were also in the cafe, but Chopper didn't bother to count them. Greasers always came hanging around when word of a run was about. None of them had hogs of their own, and in place of Angel originals they wore brass-studded black leather jackets and blue jeans.

A tall, gangling and pimply youth of about 17 detached himself from the mob of Greasers and made his way over to Chopper.

'Hi Chopper. Looks like it'll be a good run,' he said with an ingratiating smile.

Chopper allowed him a grudging nod of recognition.

Mike Garman, unofficial leader of the Greasers, was worth keeping in with, if not actually accepted as a friend.

'Got a hog yet, Mike?' asked Chopper with thinly veiled sarcasm.

'Soon, Man - soon.' Garman gritted his teeth as he spoke. It was a delicate subject.

Chopper glanced at Mike Garman and his followers with a look of disdain. They were kids - punks - but they represented the next generation of Angels, whether he liked it or not. Today's Greaser needed only a hog to put him into the two-wheeled world of the Angels. After the acquisition of a motorcycle, there would only be the initiation ceremony and the donning of originals before they became affiliated to an Angel chapter. Then, thought Chopper grimly, there might be trouble...because the kids seemed to be growing up tougher and harder as each year passed. Their values of life and property grew gradually less and their attitude to the world around them became more and more violent. To them, perhaps Angelhood meant little or nothing more than excitement. Chopper chose to see the Angels as a way of life...Garman and his bunch saw it only as a glamorous way to indulge in sex and violence.

There was a difference...a slight one, admittedly, but a difference nevertheless.

'Any chance of grabbing a ride?' asked Garman hopefully.

'On the run? Not a hope,' snapped Chopper quickly. No Angel in his right mind would take one of these kids pillion when there was a possibility of real action.

For a fleeting part of a second, Chopper half-recognised a buried thought deep in his mind which held the clue to Big M's gradual departure from the Angels, but his conscious mind refused to examine it and pushed it out angrily.

Life was the Hells Angels. There was only that...or the miserable existence of a pig citizen. a lousy choice to have to make for someone who couldn't belong to either world.

The Greasers belonged to neither. Too rebellious by nature to be swallowed into the system, they lived a half-life as apprentice Angels, waiting for the big day when they had enough money to buy a bike and enough guts to face an Angel initiation ceremony. Until then, they just hung around trying to be friendly with Angels, and hoped for a piece of the action to fall their way.

Chopper noticed Freaky hovering about over by the serving counter. He pushed past Garman and made his way over.

'Hiya feller,' said Freaky as Chopper walked up. 'Pretty good turnout, eh?' He gestured vaguely around the Greek's.

'Yeah - not bad at all,' Chopper agreed. 'Lot of new faces about.'

Freaky grinned hugely.

'It's been a long time since we was all together,' he said. 'Bound to be new faces in a couple of months.'

'Yeah.' Chopper nodded his head in agreement, whilst still

surveying the scene around him.

'Big M ain't shown up yet,' pointed out Freaky as though reading Chopper's thoughts.

'He'll be here,' said Chopper confidently. It was unthinkable that Marty wouldn't come the night before a big run.

'Maybe,' said Freaky, and Chopper plainly read the dubious note in his voice. He realised that Freaky was a potential ally if and when the time came.

Irish Mick and Danny the Deathlover sauntered over.

'Want a coffee, Man?' asked Danny.

Chopper nodded.

'Thanks.'

'Hey, Nick.' Danny leaned across the counter. 'Give us four coffees, will ya.'

The coffees came up, filled to their chipped brims and slopping over the counter and floor.

'Careful, ya crazy Greek bastard,' snapped Danny angrily. 'You'll ruin my clothes.'

He grinned and turned to the others for appreciation at his joke. Chopper and Freaky smiled indulgently. Any jokes about clothes were funny when an Angel was wearing his originals. A good set of originals boasted stains of urine, vomit, blood and beer - washing them was out of the question.

Irish Mick started telling a lurid story about the sexual appetites of his new sheep. Over to Chopper's left, someone he had never seen before was discussing the merits of Nortons and Triumphs with Adolph and Screwball Sam. All round him, people were laughing, joking and talking in high, excited voices. It was a good scene. The smell of a run was in the air and everyone was happy.

Only Nick the Greek looked as expressionless as ever. Perhaps he realised that he would have a weekend without any trade at all, or perhaps he even felt relieved at the brief respite. Either way, his face looked the same way as ever.

Chopper walked slowly around the cafe, saying hello to those he knew and asking questions about those he didn't. Passing one crowded table, a hand sneaked up behind him and gripped him firmly under the crotch.

'Hi, Chopper.'

He turned round. It was Samantha, sitting at a table with a group of four Angels Chopper had never seen before. He hadn't noticed her in the crowd.

'Taking me up back on the run?' she asked sweetly. Chopper nodded by way of assent.

'Sure, Sammy.'

He had to take a chick on the run. Samantha would do better than most. She was game for anything which was likely to transpire, and attractive enough to gain him precious class in the eyes of the others.

'Hey, listen, Man...you ought to meet these guys here,' said Sammy, waving her hand at the four Angels sat around her.

'Fellers - this is Chopper Harris, number two in this chapter.'

The four Angels mumbled an acknowledgement.

'Chopper - you'd better meet Trucker, Sam the Spick, Pee Wee Pete and Ethel. Ethel is the leader of this chapter from Dagenham. They want to bring a few of their boys along on the run.'

Chopper looked down at Ethel.

He was at least six foot three, heavy and muscular with his height and with lank, dark hair which hung down almost to his waist.

Chopper held out a hand. Ethel took it and shook it firmly.

'Hello, feller.'

'Hi, Man.'

'So what's about it? Can we bust in on your run?'

Chopper waved his hands in the air apologetically.

'Ain't for me to say, feller,' he said. 'Big M will have to give you approval for that - but I don't see why not. The more the merrier as far as I'm concerned.'

Ethel nodded vacantly.

'Sure,' he said. 'Only where is your top man tonight?'

'He'll be along later,' said Chopper, although he was already beginning to doubt it. He sneaked a look at his watch. It was nearly ten-thirty already.

'It should be a good run,' said Sammy enthusiastically.

Chopper nodded. 'Yeah - a real mind-snapper,'he answered, but his mind was already wandering off along paths which he had trodden too frequently in recent weeks. Where in the name of Hell was Marty? What did he think he was playing at? It was bad enough to let down his own chapter, but to show such bad class in front of outsiders was unforgivable.

He tried to forget about these thoughts by engaging Ethel in conversation.

'What hog you got, Man?'

Ethel shrugged.

'Harley-D...what else?'

'Yeah, of course.' Chopper smiled.

'You?'

'Bonneville...stripped and fitted with bell chargers.'

'Good machines,' Ethel grunted condescendingly.

'Yeah - not bad.'

'Wanna buy it?'

Chopper looked at Ethel in amazement.

'You kidding?...the Harley?'

'Yeah. Interested?'

Chopper sucked in air through his teeth. Of course he was interested in a Harley-Davidson.

'You bet,' he said, trying not to sound over-enthusiastic. 'What you getting rid of it for?'

Ethel shrugged.

'Got a chance to pick up an Ariel Square Four,' he said. 'They was a good hog.'

'Depends on your choice,' said Chopper. Personally, he didn't care much for the big 1000cc engine and the tuning problems that the four cylinders brought with them.

'How much d'you want for it?'

Ethel pursed his lips reflectively.

'Dunno...maybe about three-eighty...and I'll throw in the Bible.'

'If you want to do it on the cheap, he'll flog you the Bible for a hundred and throw in a Honda,' cackled the blonde-haired Angel they called Trucker. Chopper laughed politely.

'Y'know, I was once offered twenty quid for that manual,' murmured Ethel distantly. 'Not a bad offer for a Bible, was it?'

Chopper looked at him dubiously. Ten quid might be offered for a Harley-Davidson workshop manual in good condition, but twenty was a bit strong.

'They'd have to be crazy,' he said. 'You can send to the States and have one sent over for four quid.'

Ethel looked hurt.

'Not one like this you couldn't,' he said. 'It's got 'San Francisco Fuzz Department' stamped all over it.'

Chopper looked suitably impressed.

'Ex-Police bike, eh?'

'Yep,' said Ethel proudly.

Samantha looked at Chopper dreamily.

'How about that for class,' she breathed.

Chopper thought about it carefully.

'Yeah - how about that?' he echoed distantly. His thoughts were already miles away. In his mind's eyes he was roaring down the M1 on a black and white Harley-D, the speedo quivering around the magic 120 figure and the wind whistling in his ears.

Far behind him came Marty, left to breathe in his exhaust fumes as Chopper raced into the lead...and into leadership.

Chopper couldn't believe his ears. Here he was being offered the chance of a hog which could outclass Big M and outrun just about any other bike on the road...all for three hundred and eighty quid. It was a dream, and yet one which was well within the realms of possibility. He could raise three-fifty on his Triumph with little trouble. It was only a few months old.

'Hey, listen, Man...are you really serious?' he said to Ethel, half expecting him to burst into laughter as though it were all a vicious joke.

'Yes, if you're interested,' replied Ethel. 'Only it'd have to be cash on the button.'

'You'll bring it with you on the run?'

'Man - we ain't even officially invited yet,' Ethel pointed out.

Chopper gritted his teeth.

'As from right now you're invited,' he snapped firmly. 'I say so.'

Ethel looked at him quizzically. 'Can you do that, Man?'

Chopper grinned.

'I just did it,' he replied. 'If Big M wants to make the arrangements, he should be here when it's happening.'

Ethel nodded. 'Yeah - that's bad class, Man.'

Pee Wee Pete stood up.

'I vote we make some action,' he said suddenly.

'Bloody good idea,' seconded Trucker.

Chopper nodded his head in assent.

'There certainly ain't anything else happening around here,' he said, glancing at his watch.

It was eleven o'clock. Marty wasn't going to show up, of that he was now convinced.

'Be my guest,' he invited Ethel. 'Got any bright ideas and we'll fall in with you.'

Ethel looked pensive for a couple of seconds.

'What say we go and snap a few minds in Piccadilly?' he suggested. 'We'll suck eggs off the pavement, maybe rough up a few Hippies and have some fun with the queers.'

Trucker and Pee Wee laughed happily at this suggestion.

'Yeah, that's a good blast,' said Pee Wee. Then, turning to Chopper, he looked for the nod of approval.

'Tell you what, Man - last time we sucked eggs, we had this old lady who got so sick she flashed all over the pavement,' he recounted as though to finally sell the idea.

Chopper grinned. Sucking raw smashed eggs off the pavement was certainly not an original Angel trick, but it rarely failed in its purpose of snapping a few citizen minds.

'Hey, Nick.' Chopper shouted across the din in the small cafe. 'Got a coupla dozen eggs we can take away?'

Nick waved his hands wildly in the air. The signal, coming from a Greek, could have meant anything. In this case, it was a negative answer. With deliberate, exaggerated calm, he sauntered up to the table and made a great show of clearing away the empty coffee cups.

'Coffee I got...plenty of tea I got...cokes, even. But eggs I don't got,' he muttered pointedly. 'You want another coffee maybe?'

'No coffee, Nick,' said Chopper.

Nick shrugged his shoulders in a gesture of acceptance. He had tried a bit of salesmanship, and what more could a man do?

'Looks like the eggs are out,' said Chopper.

'It don't matter, Man,' said Ethel. 'I got a few other ideas...let's go down to 'Dilly anyway.'

'OK. I'll just have a word with the boys.'

Chopper strolled over to where Danny the Deathlover, Max

and Freaky were sitting at a corner table.

'Colleague over here suggests some action tonight,' he said to Danny. 'Thought it might be a nice idea if we ran along with them.'

'What's on, Man?' Freaky wanted to know. Chopper gave him a brief run down the general idea, pointing out that eggs were not part of the programme.

'Sounds like a bit of a laugh,' agreed Freaky grudgingly.

Danny the Deathlover shook his head slowly.

'Ain't you forgetting something, Chop?' he asked. 'We've gotta wait for Big M to show up. There's a lot of organising left to do for tomorrow.'

'No, I'm not forgetting...but I think Marty has,' Chopper replied bluntly. He gestured to his watch.

'Man, he'll be here,' said Danny.

Chopper gave him a wry grin.

'I wish I shared your confidence, Danny,' he said. 'The way I see it, Marty has found something better to do.'

'So he'll be along later,' said Danny. 'We can't just blow out without waiting for him.'

'OK - Please yourself,' snapped Chopper abruptly. 'I'm really fucked up with waiting around. Anybody who wants to come along is welcome. Otherwise I'll see you here in the morning, about eight-thirty.'

He waited for a few seconds.

'Well, is anyone coming?'

Freaky fidgeted nervously.

'Danny's right, you know, Chopper. We didn't ought to leave without giving Big M the chance to show up.'

'How about you, Max?'

Max shrugged. 'I think Marty would get mad,' he muttered apologetically. 'I'll wait around for a while.'

'Yeah, come on, Man. Hang around for a bit, will you?' pleaded Danny. 'Have a cup of coffee.'

'I need something stronger than coffee,' Chopper snapped. 'I need exactly what the rest of you guys need...some bloody action.'

'There'll be all the action we need tomorrow,' Danny argued. 'No sense in fucking that up just for a little piss-around tonight.'

Chopper could see that he was on his own.

'OK,' he said. 'If Big M shows up, tell him I'll be here first thing in the morning.'

'Yeah. Will do,' muttered Danny.

The subject was closed. Chopper turned to leave and hesitated. On an afterthought, he turned back to Danny the Deathlover. It might be good politics to end the conversation on a more friendly note.

'By the way - how did you make out with Doreen the other night?' he asked. 'Did she give you her 'special'?'

Danny let out a guffaw of laughter.

'Hey, Man - what a balls,' he said with a grin. 'She was waving the flag.'

Chopper smiled back.

'You should have gone for your redwings, Man,' he said.

Danny spread his hands expansively and rolled his eyes in mock sorrow.

'Didn't have no witnesses, Man,' he said, and burst into laughter again. Max and Freaky joined in. The balance was restored to a more normal level.

Chopper cut out while the going was good.

'See you,' he said as he turned on his heel.

'Yeah - be a good Angel,' said Danny.

Chopper stuck one thumb in the air. 'I'm one hundred per cent a one-percenter,' he said. It was a suitably smart crack to leave company with.

He walked back over to Ethel and his cronies.

'Looks like the boys aren't too keen on a hit tonight,' he explained, '...But I'm in if you still think it's worth it.'

Ethel always thinks it's worth it,' said Trucker. Pee Wee just grinned stupidly.

'OK with me,' said Ethel. 'Maybe it's just as well. The four of us won't attract so much fuzz attention.'

'Hey - what about me?' asked Samantha, clutching at Chopper's arm. 'Aren't you going to take me along?'

'Sorry, babe...no room,' said Chopper curtly. 'You'd just be in the way.'

Sammy pouted. 'What about later?' she asked.

'What about it?' Chopper repeated.

Samantha drew in her breath, pushing her breasts out underneath her light blue sweater.

'You know damn well what I mean,' she said pointedly.

Chopper grinned. 'What makes you think I'm interested?'

Sammy pulled at his arm teasingly.

'I didn't do so badly the other night, did I?' she wanted to know.

Chopper nodded.

'Here,' he said, fishing in his pocket and pulling out a bunch of keys. 'Let yourself into the flat and wait for me. If I'm not back in a couple of hours, start without me.'

He threw the keys in the air. Samantha caught them expertly and twisted them round her fingers reflectively.

'See you later,' she murmured slyly as Chopper walked out of the cafe with Ethel and his boys.

The Harley was parked round the corner. Chopper's heart gave a little leap as he set eyes on it for the first time. It had been stripped right down, the mudguards were off and ape-hanger handlebars put in. The front wheel forks had been extended, and expensive looking chromium-plate job done on the petrol tank and rear forks.

The only thing which marred its appearance was the repainting job which someone had done upon most of the bodywork. In place of the original black and white paintwork, the frame bore a heavy coating of shocking pink.

...But Chopper wasn't really interested in its outward appearance. Even under twenty coats of paint, he could recognise a Harley. He looked at it carefully, seeing it not as it was, but as it could be when he was in the saddle...restored to its original condition and raring to be let loose on a nice long straight stretch of road.

It was love, and desire all in one quick meeting.

The Harley was his, or soon would be. Only a few simple arrangements separated him from his dream.

Ethel grinned as Chopper stood admiring the machine.

'We got a deal?' he asked.

Chopper nodded. 'I think we got a deal,' he said with finality. 'But I'd like to give her a run-around to check a few points.'

'No time like now, Man,' said Ethel, and threw him the keys. 'Where's yours?'

Chopper gestured round the corner of the alleyway.

'Blue and white job, flying a crossbones pennant,' he said. He fished in his pocket and pulled out his keys. Ethel disappeared round the corner in search of the Triumph.

Chopper straddled the Harley-Davidson gingerly, sliding back and forth on the seat until the foot pedals were in the correct position. Turning the ignition key, he rose in the saddle and plunged the kick-starter down viciously. The big engine turned over a couple of times, coughed and failed. He pulled back the throttle another half an inch and tried again. This time the engine fired, and revved somewhat lumpily. Chopper throttled back a few times experimentally.

The engine was way out of tune, he decided. It needed a bit of work before it would give of its best, but the steady throb of power under his legs reminded Chopper just how good that best could be.

He pulled the bike upright from the kerb, snapped up the footrest with his heel and slid the machine into first gear. Pulling away, he swung the hog round in a wide U-turn and went after Ethel.

Ethel looked at him, waved a thumbs-up signal and roared away.

'Meet you under the Coke sign,' he shouted over this shoulder as he disappeared round the bend. Trucker and Pee Wee had already left. Chopper swung the bike after them and pulled back the throttle.

It took him only a matter of seconds to catch up. A hundred yards or so ahead he saw the tail lights of his Triumph. Changing down gear and pulling back the throttle, Chopper marvelled at the ease with which he closed the gap and came up alongside Ethel.

'Good hog,' he shouted across above the roar of the two bikes.

'Yeah - not bad,' Ethel agreed, and pulled back his throttle viciously. The Triumph leapt forward with a snarl.

Chopper was right on his trail. As the two bikes surged forward, Chopper saw the flash of a traffic signal changing from green to amber a few hundred feet ahead. He didn't hesitate for a second. Crashing the gears down, he pulled every ounce of strength out of the engine, made a couple of racing changes and headed straight for the cross-roads. Ethel had already started to slow down when Chopper shot past. The light was red several seconds before he came to it, and traffic waiting on the other road had already started to move.

In a momentary panic, Chopper wondered what his chances of stopping were. Realising that he didn't have a hope, he kept right on going.

A red Volvo sports car shot away from the lights and tried to show up a driver in a Mini-Cooper. Both cars, anticipating the green light, had been ready to move. They were both halfway across the road when Chopper reached the spot.

The Volvo kept moving, obviously expecting Chopper to veer round his back. The Mini-driver, panicking, at first tried to slam on his brakes, then suddenly changed his mind and slewed the car round to the right, directly in Chopper's path.

There was only a narrow channel between the two cars when Chopper hit the spot. He saw only one slim chance...and took it. He headed straight through the gap.

The wild gamble paid off, but only just. As he roared through, Chopper felt his right-hand footrest snick against the side panel of the Mini. The shock travelled up through his leg and into his hip. Then he was through - with no other damage than a smear of green cellulose on the foot pedal. As he roared on, Chopper could hear the Mini-driver blasting his horn furiously out of anger and fear.

Chopper slowed down to let Ethel catch up. Half a minute later, he heard the roar of the Triumph behind him, and looked briefly over his shoulder.

Ethel brought the Triumph up alongside. He was grinning murderously, and the look was tinged with more than a hint of admiration.

A warm glow of contentment flooded through Chopper. He had scored valuable points in the class war...to earn admiration from a chapter leader. He allowed himself to smile gently.

They cruised the rest of the way together - now firm friends by virtue of the machines they shared an interest in. Trucker and Pee Wee were waiting for them when they arrived.

Chopper dismounted first, and offered Ethel back his ignition key.

'Thanks,' he said simply.

'Right then,' said Trucker. 'What's on?'

'I think we'll dump the hogs round the back of Shaftesbury Avenue,' suggested Ethel. 'Just in case the fuzz get snoopy.'

He climbed back on to his Harley and kicked the engine into life.

'Once round Eros?' shouted Pee Wee above the din as the four bikes revved noisily.

'You're on,' retorted Chopper, and shot away from the pavement with a squeal of rubber.

Chopper took great delight in carving up a taxi, scaring the life out of a young couple crossing the road and shooting an amber light on his way round. He cut through the one-way system via a couple of back alleys. The others missed the turning and had to continue down the main road.

Chopper made his way through the narrow alleyways until he came out on the road again. He waited with his engine purring quietly for the sound of the other bikes.

They were not long in coming. Chopper heard the roar of three powerful engines cutting up the heavy London traffic as they came towards him. Judging his move to the precise second, he screamed out from the alleyway, cut across the path of Ethel riding neck and neck with Pee Wee and pulled back the throttle viciously. Within seconds, he had taken the lead and hit the traffic lights. Through on a green light, Chopper swung the bike round Piccadilly Circus at a breakneck speed, turning off once more into Shaftesbury Avenue.

He stopped to wait for the others. They got caught by another set of lights. A minute or so later, Ethel arrived first with Pee Wee close on his heels.

'I must say you can sure use that hog,' muttered Ethel with admiration. 'One of these days we must really have a burn-up.'

'Any time,' said Chopper, struggling to keep a straight face.

'OK - let's dump the hogs and go see the junkies,' said Ethel. He led the way round to a back-street where they parked the bikes up against the pavement and dismounted.

They walked back round to the Circus. Ethel looked all around carefully, seeking out possible trouble and looking for the best place to start some action.

Chopper pointed over to the all-night Boots chemists' shop. It was just before midnight, and already a small queue of drug addicts had built up. They waited patiently but desperately for their precious prescriptions.

'Let's go see what we can do over there,' he suggested.

'I got a better idea,' said Ethel. He led the way round to the public lavatories.

'There'll be more action here,' said Ethel pointing. 'At this time of night, the very last thing anyone goes down there for is a piss.'

Chopper laughed. He was perfectly right. The men's loo served only two purposes at present - as a meeting place for homosexuals and their pick-ups for the night and a place in which to pump that much-needed shot of heroin into hungry veins.

'You wanna roll a queer?' asked Trucker. The question was directed at Chopper.

'Don't mind...what do you think, Man?' he said to Ethel.

'Screw that,' snapped Ethel, waving the idea off with a gesture of his hands. 'I got an idea which should be a bit more rewarding for us guys who like their sex straight.'

He grinned mysteriously as the others looked at him with unspoken questions. 'Just wait and see,' he added afterwards.

They waited. Several minutes passed. A few Hippies strolled in and out of the entrance to the loo, closely followed by queers.

Ethel was obviously waiting for something...or someone.

'What you waiting for Man?' asked Chopper eventually.

Ethel smiled faintly. 'Him,' he said suddenly, and pointed to a drunken-looking Hippy staggering towards the loo. Although his movements looked awkward and fumbling, he was in a hell of a hurry and he knew exactly where he was going. He was no drunk, of that Chopper was certain.

Ethel waited until he had disappeared down the steps leading to the lavatory. 'OK,' he said and hurried towards the entrance.

Chopper ran after him, with Pee Wee and Trucker on his heels.

They hurried down the steps, and were just in time to see the Hippy disappear into a cubicle and lock it behind him.

Ethel looked around carefully. The place was otherwise empty.

'Quick,' he snapped suddenly. 'You and Pee Wee go outside and keep a look out for fuzz,' he snapped to Trucker, 'Chopper - follow me.'

With that he ran straight towards the cubicle door, jumping up at the last second and scaling the door. he pulled himself up on top of the door and dropped through on the other side. A surprised shout preceded a quick scream of pain by a split second. The bolt was drawn back and Ethel opened the door.

'Quick,' he whispered to Chopper, beckoning with his finger.

Chopper ran into the cubicle and Ethel slammed the door shut behind him.

The Hippy sat back on the toilet seat with blood dribbling from one corner of his mouth. His eyes, already wild-looking with the drug-craving, now looked even worse with fear. In his trembling fingers, he held a hypodermic syringe and a small packet.

Ethel snatched the packet of drugs from him and knocked the syringe to the floor. With savage glee, he stamped on it with his heavy boot, powdering the broken glass on the hard stone floor.

All remaining life seemed to leak out of the sick-looking junkie. With a low moan, he rolled back even further and slid down the wall of the toilet to the ground. He lay there twitching for a few seconds while Ethel carefully tucked the drugs into his pockets and reached behind him for the door catch.

'See if the coast is clear,' he whispered quietly to Chopper.

Chopper peered out of the crack in the door furtively.

'OK,' he muttered.

'Right then - out you go,' said Ethel. Chopper opened the door wider and hurried out. As he half-turned, he just saw Ethel draw back his foot and deliver a vicious kick to the junkie's ribcage. He didn't even murmur as the blow stuck home. Deprived of his drug, he was already beyond pain.

Ethel came out of the cubicle and slammed the door behind him.

'Let's go,' he said walking casually towards the exit.

They walked out and up the stone steps. Pee Wee and Trucker waited for them at the top. Ethel looked all round as they came out to the street and waved his head to them to follow him. He ran across the road, narrowly avoiding a couple of cars.

'Hey Man - you don't use that stuff, do you?' asked Chopper when they had regained the safety of the pavement.

Ethel laughed. 'No, I don't,' he said. 'But around here it ain't hard to find someone who does.'

Chopper waited a few seconds for further explanation, but none was forthcoming.

He followed meekly as Ethel walked round the Circus to the queue outside Boots.

Ethel stopped, looked and waited. It didn't take long to find what he wanted.

A young girl was accosting everyone as they came out of the chemists.

Each time she was answered with a rapid shake of the head, or a rude gesture.

Chopper looked at her face. She was not bad looking, but more than a little ravaged by the effects of the drug she was undoubtedly addicted to. She looked hopeless, desperate and frightened.

Ethel headed straight for her.

'Hey, babe,' he whispered to her.

The girl turned, her face brightening for a second with a look of sudden hope. It died just as suddenly as she focused her glazed eyes upon Ethel. She was hoping for one of the pushers she knew - and Ethel didn't look likely at all.

She went to turn away again. Ethel fished in his pocket and pulled out the small packet of drugs in his clenched fist. He waved it very briefly under her nose.

'You wanna score, huh?' he muttered.

A flash of fire came into the girl's eyes. A stupid smile spread across her face, showing that she was indeed quite an attractive chick.

'How much?' she murmured pleadingly.

Ethel grinned at her. 'We'll talk about that later,' he said. 'Right now you look at though you could do with a little shot to keep you going...right?'

The girl nodded her head vigorously.

'OK - follow us,' said Ethel. Turning his back on her, he walked back across the road and headed for where the bikes were parked.

The girl didn't hesitate for a second. For what Ethel had in his pocket, she would have willingly followed him into Hell.

Chopper walked alongside Ethel.

'What's going on, Man?' he said in a puzzled voice. The action was progressing a little too fast for him.

'We're gonna have a bit of fun, that's all,' said Ethel with one of his wicked grins. 'The chick needs H, we need a fuck...So we do a deal.'

They arrived back at the bikes. Ethel gestured to the girl to climb up on the pillion. She did so at once.

'You got a pad?' Ethel asked her.

'Yes - Camden Town,' replied the girl with a nod.

'OK - direct me when we get there,' said Ethel and mounted the hog.

'You done this sort of thing before?' asked Chopper of Trucker as they mounted the bikes.

'Yeah - a couple of times,' said Trucker in a bored voice. 'It's a giggle, ain't it?'

'Yeah? Not for the junkie who's lost his fix.'

'He'll live,' said Trucker callously. 'Anyway - serves the stupid bastard right for getting himself hooked.'

'Yes - I suppose so,' replied Chopper as he kicked over the Triumph.

The convoy shot off up Shaftesbury Avenue, into Charing Cross road and round St Giles Circus. Ethel was racing along at breakneck speed - probably for the benefit of his pillion passenger. At the end of Tottenham Court Road, they screamed across from the right-hand lane, round a central bollard and cut across traffic to take the road to Camden Town.

The girl lived at the Kentish Town end. Ethel pulled up outside a dilapidated-looking tenement house.

'This looks like the place, fellers,' he shouted over his shoulder.

He parked the bike and followed the girl up the pathway to the porch.

The front door had no lock on it. The girl pushed the half-rotten, peeling door and it swung open to reveal a hallway ankle-deep in dust and filth. A stench of decaying food wafted through the doorway into the street.

'Follow me,' whispered the girl, heading for the uncarpeted staircase. She led the way to a brown door and once again pushed it open.

The room was fairly large, but badly furnished. It boasted only an unmade bed, with a couple of filthy blankets thrown loosely over it, a row of clothes pegs on one wall and two or three planks balanced upon bricks which served as a bookshelf and record rack.

A few colourful posters of The Rolling Stones were the only things which lent any brightness to the drab surroundings.

The girl crossed the room to the gas ring and lit the gas. She placed a small saucepan of water upon the flaming jets to boil.

'Can I have a shot now,' she pleaded.

Ethel grinned. 'We haven't discussed payment yet,' he reminded her.

The girl smiled a sad, ironic smile.

'I know what you want,' she muttered in a weary voice. 'And when I've had a shot I won't even care.'

Chopper gritted his teeth together. The poor kid looked so pathetic he felt sorry for her. He didn't like this business at all, but to say anything would be stupid.

'Here,' Ethel tossed her the tiny packet. The girl missed it and it fell to the floor. She reached down to pick it up hastily, her movements betraying the depth of her desperation.

She took it over to the gas ring and poured a small quantity into a teaspoon. Mixing it with water from the boiling saucepan, she blew on it carefully to cool it before pulling open one of the drawers and taking out a hypo.

The syringe filled, she pulled up one sleeve of her sweater to expose an arm which bore the tiny marks of a hundred such needle-pricks. Some had festered slightly leaving ugly red blotches and little scabs.

Saliva dribbled from between her lips as she plunged the needle deep into fleshy part of her arm and pushed down the plunger.

The effect was almost instantaneous and dramatic. As Chopper watched her face, she changed into another person. The tired, weary, desperate little kid died and a vibrant, vivacious young woman took her place. The girl's eyes seemed to suddenly come alive as though someone had lit electric light bulbs behind them. Her drooping shoulders straightened, and she looked two or three inches taller at once. Her dowdy looks were gone as she turned towards Chopper and Ethel and smiled gratefully. Suddenly she was a really attractive woman, with a glowing beauty which shone from the inside.

Chopper watched the change in fascination. He had never seen a junkie taking a shot before.

The girl let out a sudden burst of relieved laughter.

'Thanks,' she said, and danced across the floor to the record player lying on the floor.

She switched it on and chose a couple of LPs from a small pile. She put them on and a burst of strange electronic music filled the room. She continued dancing, in vague time to the strange sounds, and every part of her body seemed to be fluid and mobile.

'OK you bastards,' she screamed suddenly in a loud voice. 'Help yourselves.'

With that she pulled off her sweater and tugged at the fastener on her skirt. She shrugged out of her bra and panties and stood before them utterly naked.

Chopper looked at her body appreciatively. She had a good figure, although the effects of her addiction had left their marks. She was much thinner than she should have been for her height, and her breast seemed to droop heavily. Underneath her breasts, her ribs showed sharply through her flesh. Her hips, however, were firm, and well-rounded and as she pirouetted round Chopper noticed that she had a small, well shaped bottom and nice legs.

Ethel peeled off his denim jacket and tugged at the zipper of his jeans.

'After me fellers,' he said, and advanced on the girl slowly. He grabbed her by the arm and pulled her on to the bed.

Chopper watched dispassionately as Ethel hauled himself over on to her prone body and started to thrust against her. The scene was having its expected effect on him and he felt his stomach tighten with sexual arousal. He thought momentarily of Samantha waiting back in his flatlet for him and then his mind strayed to similar thoughts of Elaine.

The girl stripping off her clothes like that had reminded him of Elaine the other night. Chopper licked his dry lips as he thought of her lush young body flaunted in front of him. He grinned to himself as he pictured himself plunging into her on his bed as Marty looked on in silence.

The dream was so vivid, he was hardly aware of Trucker and Pee Wee taking their turns on the bed with the girl.

Ethel was prodding him in the back.

'Well, go on, Man. She's all yours.'

Chopper snapped back to reality and the situation which faced him. Dumbly, like an automaton, he strolled over to where the girl lay motionless and climbed up onto the bed beside her.

For a moment he paused as he looked into the girl's eyes. She was staring up at him blankly, her mind far away in her own private world, but a sardonic, mocking little smile played about the corners of her mouth. Chopper stared, bewildered, as the face went misty, dissolved and finally reappeared as Elaine's face, smiling up at him.

He pulled hastily at his jeans, pulled up his shirt and straddled her. He satisfied himself quickly, and roughly, like an animal.

'OK fellers...let's go,' called Ethel as soon as Chopper had climbed off the girl and zipped himself up. He was already half-way through the door before Chopper had finished tucking in his shirt.

'Hey - Ethel...give the kid the rest of the stuff,' said Chopper, knowing that Ethel had picked it up from where the girl had left it.

Ethel paused for a moment, then shrugged.

'Yeah - why not?' he said and fished in his pocket.

'Here,' he called to the girl, and tossed the packet across the room towards her. It fell a few feet short of the bed. The girl didn't move.

'She'll find it when she wants it,' laughed Ethel. 'When these bastards need a shot, they can sniff it out in a pile of shit.'

He ducked out of the door, closely followed by Pee Wee and Trucker.

Chopper looked back at the girl once before leaving the room. She was laying as still as death, with the same stupid, dreamy smile on her face.

Chopper closed the door quietly behind him and followed the others down the stairs.

Samantha was fast asleep in his single bed when Chopper let himself into his room. He undressed quietly and climbed in beside her. She stirred a couple of times, muttered something under her breath, but didn't wake up.

Chopper lay awake for quite a long time before finally dropping off. The last thing he thought of before falling asleep was the run planned for the next morning. He wondered whether Big M had shown up at the Greek's.

'Good morning,' said Samantha brightly, thrusting a steaming cup of coffee under his nose.

Chopper blinked a couple of times and tried to shake the early-morning muzziness out of his head. He peered blearily at his watch.

'Christ, it's early,' he cursed. It was only twenty to seven.

'Big day,' said Samantha.

Chopper sat bolt upright in bed and snatched the coffee out of her hand. He placed it on the floor and grabbed Samantha round the waist, pulling her down on to the bed.

'Randy bastard,' said Sammy with a grin as he slid his fingers under her tights. '...But seeing as how I had to play with myself last night...' Her voice trailed off as she felt beneath the bedclothes.

'Get your clothes off,' Chopper muttered anxiously. 'We've only got time for a quick one.'

Samantha pouted playfully as she hurriedly climbed out of her clothes.

'One of these days, Chopper, you're going to really make a woman out of me,' she teased.

He didn't answer, but got straight down to the business in hand with no preliminaries.

Afterwards they sat on the edge of the bed and smoked a cigarette with their cold coffee.

'What's the time?' asked Samantha. Chopper glanced at his watch.

'Seven-fifteen,' he said, and swung his legs over to the other side of the bed. Reaching to the floor, he picked up his jeans and pulled them on.

He crossed the room to the washbasin and splashed cold water over his face.

51

'What time are the boys meeting in the Greek's?' Samantha wanted to know.

Chopper dried his face on a dingy towel.

'About half-eight, I should think.' He peered closely at his face in the mirror wondering whether to shave or not. The heavy black stubble looked quite promising, he thought. Perhaps he ought to grow a beard.

'Reckon I ought to grow a beard?' he called to Samantha.

'Please yourself.'

Chopper looked at his reflection and tried to imagine himself with a thick, luxurious growth. He thought of his attempt to grow a beard two years previously. It had looked quite promising for the first two weeks, then had deteriorated into a patchy and untidy mess. The trouble with trying to grow a beard was that people laughed if it didn't quite come off. He thought carefully for a few seconds and decided not to risk it.

'Fuck it...beards are too common,' he snapped, and reached for his razor.

It was a quarter to eight by the time he had finished grooming himself for the run. His black leather boots had been painstakingly polished until they shone brilliantly. The helmet too, had been rubbed with metal polish and a soft cloth until it gave off a dull glow. He fished in a drawer and pulled out every piece of armament and jewellery he could find.

Finally, he went to the food cupboard and extracted a small package of silver cooking foil. He looked inside it, appraising the amount of hashish it contained. There was enough for five or six good heavy joints. He tucked the packet in his top pocket together with a packet of liquorice cigarette papers.

'OK,' he said. 'Let's go.'

On the way to the Greek's, Chopper wondered what to do if Marty hadn't shown up. He thought over the possibilities carefully and examined every possible angle and situation.

If Marty did fail to show up, Chopper might be expected to cancel the run. However, if he organised it in Big M's absence, he would stand a good chance of earning himself a bit of class.

He analysed this possibility more closely, and realised that he secretly hoped Marty would fail to appear.

Arriving outside the Greek's, Chopper looked around carefully for Marty's hog. It was nowhere in sight. He dismounted, and walked into the cafe with Samantha trailing behind him.

Not many of the boys had shown up yet. Chopper noted Danny the Deathlover, Max and Irish Mick. A few others were clustered over in a corner and several of the Angel birds sat around the tables looking tired and drinking coffee. A heavy contingent of Greasers were also present - no doubt still hanging on in the hopes of scrounging a ride.

Chopper pointed over to Doreen and three other Angel birds.

'Go and sit with the birds,' he commanded Sammy. 'I'm gonna have a word with the boys.'

She obeyed meekly. Chopper strolled over to Danny.

'Well, what's the score?' he asked. 'Has Big M been in touch?'

Danny shook his head. He looked quite worried.

'We waited until nearly one o'clock last night,' he said. 'He hadn't shown up by then so we blew.'

'What do you reckon, Chop?' asked Irish Mick. 'Do you reckon someone ought to shoot round to his pad and find out what's happening?'

'If anyone's gonna go it'd better be Chopper,' said Danny. 'What about it Chop?'

Chopper shrugged. 'He'll be here if he wants to be here,' he said. 'I'm not his fucking alarm clock, am I?'

Irish Mick grinned nervously. Danny the Deathlover's face remained impassive.

'Something may have happened,' he pointed out.

'Yeah - something's happened all right,' snapped Chopper darkly, and caught the accusing look in Danny's eyes. 'Sod it - right now I want a coffee.'

He walked up to the counter and ordered it. Nick nodded his head faintly by way of acknowledgement.

'You boys out for some trouble today, huh?' he queried.

Chopper looked at him with mock horror on his face.

'Trouble, Nick?...Us?' he said with a sneer.

Nick took the money for the coffee and turned his back. Conversation wasn't Nick's strong point.

'Hey - here's Big M,' called Max's voice. Chopper looked outside. Elaine was just climbing off the back of Marty's bike as he parked it against the kerb. He looked somewhat sheepish as he strolled in.

'Christ, sorry I didn't make it last night, fellers,' he said apologetically, walking straight up to Chopper and Danny. 'I had a spot of bother.'

'Yeah? What sort of bother Man?' asked Danny anxiously.

'Forget it - it's not important,' said Marty hurriedly, trying to pass it all off quickly.

'Sure it's important,' Danny argued. 'If you've been in bother, then we want to know it...don't we fellers?' He turned to the others for confirmation.

Irish Mick and Max nodded their heads enthusiastically with agreement.

'Yeah - what was the trouble, Marty?' asked Chopper.

'Well, it wasn't a rumble or anything like that,' muttered Marty awkwardly. Chopper could see he didn't really want to talk about it.

'It was the hog,' said Elaine suddenly, answering for him. 'The bloody thing broke down on us, didn't it?'

Marty flashed her an angry look.

'Yeah - we was out Epping Forest way, and the throttle cable snapped,' he admitted sheepishly. 'I was going to get back here for about half-past nine, but as it was we had to push the hog nearly eight miles to a garage. Time we got back it was too bloody late so I thought we'd come straight down this morning.'

'Oh, well...it couldn't be helped, could it?' murmured Max understandingly, but his voice didn't ring true. Chopper smiled inwardly. Big M had just hammered another nail into the coffin of his dwindling leadership.

Chopper knew exactly what the others were thinking - much the same as he was. No hog was perfect, nothing which consisted of mechanical parts could ever be one hundred per cent reliable - and breakdowns and accidents could never be completely avoided.

...But Big M was an Angel. His hog was a two-wheeled god, and was supposed to be treated as such. It was bad class to let a stupid thing like a breakdown occur the night before a run. Any righteous Angel gave his hog a really thorough going over at least three days before any full-scale action was planned. Marty had made a bad mistake - he had shown himself to be out of touch with the really important things.

Marty sensed the general air of disapproval, and was about ready to move away when Chopper spotted Ethel and a crowd of Angels from his chapter strolling in through the door.

Chopper confronted Marty.

'By the way, Man, a few of the guys from Dagenham were in last night,' he said. 'They asked me if they could run with us, and as you weren't around I invited 'em along. Thought it would help to add strength.'

Marty glanced at him piercingly for a fleeting second. He was thrown, off balance and unsure of himself, and he recognised a fait accompli when he saw one.

'Yeah - great,' he mumbled without much enthusiasm. There wasn't really much else he could say.

Ethel saw Chopper and headed over. His eyes flicked over the group, quickly identifying Marty as the leader. Observing protocol, he ignored Chopper and held out his hand to Marty.

'Hi, Man. they call me Ethel...from Dagenham.'

Marty took the proffered handshake.

'Marty Gresham...Big M,' he murmured. 'I hear you're gonna run with us?'

Ethel grinned. 'That's right, Man. I checked it out with Chopper last night.' He smiled at Chopper for the first time, 'Hi Chop.'

'Yeah - that's cool,' said Marty. 'How many boys you got with you?'

Ethel gestured to the bunch trailing behind him. Chopper recognised Trucker, Pee Wee and Sam the Spick. There were three others.

'Pee Wee, Trucker, Mudso, Sam the Spick, Frenchie and Grass,' he said as he introduced them. 'Only seven of us, but Grass is worth four when it comes to participating.'

Chopper appraised Grass and believed it. He stood a good six foot two, carried around thirteen stones of well-proportioned muscle and boasted fists like clubs.

'Mind you, fighting's about all he is good for,' continued

Ethel with a good natured grin. 'Grass rides a hog like a prick, and rides a woman like a dog.'

Grass grinned stupidly. 'Why fuck when you can fight?' he muttered in a gruff voice.

'So where's the run, Man?' asked Ethel.

Marty shrugged.

'One coast town's as good as another, ain't it?' he said. 'Thought it might be a good hit to make Bournemouth.'

Ethel pursed his lips and shook his head disapprovingly.

'You been there recently?' he asked. It was a loaded question.

'No, not for a few months,' admitted Marty grudgingly, 'What's with it?'

'Bad scene,' said Ethel, still shaking his head. 'The fuzz are pretty uptight these days. We was down there only a month ago, and three of our boys got busted.'

Marty glanced at Chopper.

'What do you think, Chopper?'

Chopper thought about it for a time. 'I reckon we ought to hit somewhere smaller,' he said eventually. 'A little place where they're not used to Angel raiding parties. Somewhere we can really blow a few minds.'

'Got anywhere in mind?' asked Marty.

'How about one of the smaller Cornish towns?' suggested Sam the Spick helpfully.

'Too far,' pointed out Marty and Ethel almost simultaneously.

Chopper racked his brains. The germ of an idea came to him.

'I've got it,' he said brightly. 'Seaford...that's the place.'

Chopper grinned maliciously to himself as he thought about it. He owed the sleepy little seaside resort of Seaford a favour of long standing. The last time he had ever been forced to accompany his parents on holiday had been a fortnight in the place. Even though it was many years previously, Chopper could still remember those fourteen boring days and nights. By day it had poured with rain, and by night he had been forced to seek excitement in penny slot machine arcades and sickening coffee bars full of pigs wearing 'kiss-me-quick' hats.

Yes, he thought to himself, Seaford certainly deserved a visit of revenge.

Marty considered the idea thoughtfully.

'Yeah, could be good,' he mused. 'Straight down the M4 as far as we can go, along the A4, through Bristol and Bath...we could make it in just over three hours. Not too long and not too short either. Could be a good run.'

'Tell you something else,' put in Ethel, as he warmed to the idea. 'I know where the hangout of the Bristol chapter is...we could pop in and maybe pick up a few of the boys from there on the way down.'

Chopper's eyes sparkled brighter as he thought of it. This could be a really big one...the sort of run which the original Hells Angels in the USA would have been proud of. Angel folklore still told of the legendary run on Monterey, California, when more than 200 Angels had descended on the town for three days of riot, rape and raving it up.

'OK?' called Marty. The entire clientele of the Greek's shouted an affirmative answer. With screams, whoops and much scraping of chairs on the floor, the crowded cafe emptied into the street outside.

Nick, phlegmatic as ever, looked at the departing horde, shrugged philosophically, threw a greasy tea-towel over one shoulder and started to clear up the debris the Angels had left behind.

As the roar of hogs outside filled the air Nick wondered vaguely if he ought to take the wife and kids to the coast for a couple of days. He wouldn't do much business this weekend, and he needed a holiday anyway.

Bournemouth ought to be nice at his time of year, he mused thoughtfully....Safe too.

The noise of the departing bikes faded into the distance.

The invasion of the small holiday town of Seaford started at two-fifteen in the afternoon. The local residents first knew of their singular honour when half a dozen hogs raced up through the main shopping centre towards the sea front.

It had been a good, clean fast run, with little trouble other than the odd breakdown. Big M led the first wave of riders triumphantly through the town like the vanguard of some all-conquering band of heroes. Behind him rode Chopper, Freaky, Danny the Deathlover, Irish Mick and Grass. The others lay behind them, strung out along the road according to the power of their hogs and their degree of riding skill. Ethel and a couple of his boys had dropped off along the way to see what reinforcements they could raise in Bristol.

The promenade had already been nominated as the gathering-place. Big M pulled up beside the sea wall and switched off his engine. Elaine dismounted and ran to look over the beach.

'Who's for a swim?' she cried excitedly. There were no immediate takers.

Grass sniffed in deeply.

'Hey, Man...dig that sea air,' he shouted exultantly. 'Let's kick these pigs off the beach so there's more of it to go round.'

Big M smiled indulgently.

'Cool it Man,' he said softly. 'We'll wait until everyone arrives.'

They waited.

Over the next hour, the Angels arrived in groups. The last stragglers cruised into town before three o'clock, massed together with the rest along the promenade and waited expectantly. There was a strong sense of tension in the air - an almost tangible vibration of repressed violence which threatened to burst out at any second. There was little action, except for a few Angels shouting obscene remarks or making threatening gestures to any holidaymakers who stared a little too intently at them.

Chopper looked at the long line of Nazi helmets glinting in the bright sunlight and at the glistening chrome of the hogs. Then he looked at the puzzled, frightened, unsure faces of the holiday crowds and smiled broadly. A feeling of sheer pride

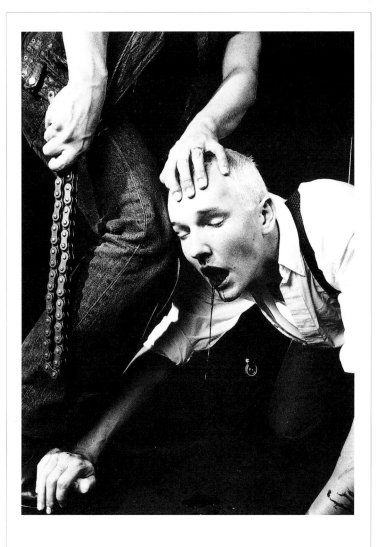

Concept / Art Direction — Nigel Wingrove
Photography — Chris Bell
Hair and Make up — Ashley Mae
Models: — Chopper — Crock   **Mama —** Heather
Biker Girl — Linsey   **Biker —** Paul   **Man —** Georgio
All pictures posed by models — ie don't try this at home

surged through him. This was what Angelhood was all about; this was the true power and magnificence of the Hells Angels.

When Ethel finally turned up with a dozen riders from Bristol, it was time for a count of heads.

Big M walked slowly along the promenade mentally counting the silent, yet menacing throng. He beamed with satisfaction at his small army. There was forty-eight riders and thirty chicks...a formidable battalion of Hell-raisers against any local police force.

Big M sauntered along the line and walked with exaggerated coolness back to his hog.

'OK,' he shouted over his shoulder as he kicked the machine into life once again. 'We run.'

Wild screams and shouts burst from fifty throats behind him, and the very air vibrated with shock waves as the long line of bikes exploded into a throbbing, roaring sound of menace.

One by one, the riders peeled off from the kerb to start their parade along the sea-front. As the mob moved slowly along the road, riders pulled up into an almost regimental pattern of mechanised precision. Four-deep, the Hell's Angels set out to make their declaration to the people of Seaford.

We are here, and this town is ours.

The effect was immediate, and dramatic. The anxious crowds who had been watching became fidgety and nervous. Heads turned towards the noise of the bikes and parents rushed about collecting their children with looks of fear on their faces. Car drivers pulled off the road hurriedly and the people milling in the roadway scurried for the comparative safety of the pavements.

The Angels accelerated to a reasonable cruising speed along the promenade. For a good mile and a half, the road lay almost straight out in front of them. They flashed by, hurling insults at passers-by, came to the end of the stretch and wheeled round.

The fuzz were waiting when they made the return trip.

Two Panda cars, blue lights flashing, pulled alongside the leaders and motioned them into the kerb.

Big M raised his hand high in the air and gestured his followers to comply. The Angels pulled in, but left their engines switched on, throbbing quietly.

Two constables climbed out of each car. Quickly identifying Big M and Chopper as the official leaders, they closed in somewhat warily.

'OK boys. That's about enough now,' said one of the cops in a patronising tone.

Big M smiled at him disarmingly.

'But officer,' he said with an air of aggrieved innocence. 'We aren't causing any trouble.'

'No - just causing a general nuisance and a traffic obstruction,' snapped the copper. 'Let's keep things nice and peaceful, shall we?'

'We're just having a little holiday,' put in Chopper in the same sarcastic tone as Marty. 'A few hours in the lovely fresh seaside air.'

The cop's eyes narrowed to slits as he appraised the full strength of the mob.

'All right,' he said finally. 'We'll leave it at that for now...but just be warned. One sign of any trouble from you lot and we'll be down on you...hard.'

Seventy-odd faces smiled sweetly as the fuzz returned to their cars and drove off.

'You heard what the nice man said,' shouted Big M. 'Let's all have a nice, peaceful day by the sea.'

A chorus of laughs and whistles greeted his remark. The Angels were just beginning to warm up.

Ethel pulled up from the ranks behind.

'Hey, Man...you see what I saw back down the road there?' he asked Big M.

'No. What?'

Ethel grinned wickedly.

'A lovely big, wide-open holiday camp, that's all,' he said excitedly. 'Reckon we ought to treat ourselves to a little holiday?'

Marty glanced briefly at Chopper, who caught his eye and nodded his head thoughtfully.

'OK - let's cruise down and take a look,' he ventured.

The mob needed no second bidding. With more screams and war cries, the phalanx of riders wheeled round yet again and headed back down the road to the camp entrance.

'Hey...we've even got an invitation,' yelled Chopper, pointing to the large sign which hung outside the main gate.

It read plainly: 'Day visitors welcome.'

'What more do we need?' said Big M, peeling off the road and heading in through the gate. The others followed him in.

Just inside the gates, a security guard sat in his little hut like a sentry on guard duty. At the sound of the hogs, he leapt out and desperately tried to close the two heavy metal and wire gates.

Chopper quickly kicked down his footrest, dismounted and ran over to him. Danny the Deathlover and Big M were right behind him.

Chopper jammed his booted foot under the bottom edge of the gate.

'Now what sort of a welcome do you call this?' he asked the guard.

The security man looked at him nervously.

'You're not welcome,' he snapped with far more bravado than he felt. 'We don't want any of your type in here.'

Chopper's hand snaked out, clutching the security guard by the lapels of his uniform. His face froze into a vicious leer.

'Listen buddy...what you want and what you get are two different things,' he murmured quietly. 'Now unless you want to get yourself into some rather nasty bother, you'll just get back out of the way and smile sweetly.'

Behind him, Danny and Big M slapped their fists against their palms in a menacing gesture.

The guard got the message.

Defeated, he backed away from the gates and watched sullenly and the entourage of bikes poured in through the entrance.

As they drove in, Samantha reached out from the pillion seat of Chopper's hog and snatched the guard's cap from his head.

'Thanks, handsome,' she laughed as she placed the hat on her own head. 'Just what I always wanted.'

Chopper turned to look at her and grinned.

'Good for you, Sammy,' he said.

'OK, let's show these bastards a thing or two,' shouted Big M, and revved up his Harley.

With Elaine clinging tightly to his back, he shot off across the car park, weaving skilfully in and out of the tight lines of parked vehicles.

Within seconds, twenty riders were playing a crazy game of two-wheeled tag. The air filled with the sound of racing engines, screams and war-whoops and the scraping of metal against metal as handlebars and footrests stripped off slivers of cellulose from parked cars.

Some of the Angel birds had dismounted, and were gleefully letting down car tyres and trying to open doors and bonnets. When successful, they pulled and ripped out wiring, distributor cables and anything which would come loose. When cheated of this objective, they satisfied themselves with tearing off radio aerials and kicking dents in the bodywork.

The game lasted only a few minutes before the Angels tired of it.

There was no longer any of the earlier pretence. Big M was no longer the leader of a band of high-spirited youths. The miniature army had turned into a raiding party. The gang had become a mob, and mobs acknowledge no one leader.

Chopper looked around and grinned savagely. Big M had led them here, and now his part was done. It was every man for himself now, and the best man would show himself by showing his class. He picked out Ethel and the Bristol riders, and drove towards them.

'Hey, Ethel...let's look around a bit,' he shouted above the din.

Ethel looked over and nodded.

'Better ditch your bird,' he shouted back.

Chopper turned to Samantha. 'Hop off babe.'

Sammy shrugged, but dismounted without a word. She looked around for another hog to ride on.

'Hey, Freaky...got a ride?'

'Yeah - come on,' he said, patting the pillion seat behind him. Sammy climbed on the hog and Freaky took off in pursuit of Big M and a group of about four riders.

Chopper looked around and assessed the situation. Big M had taken Freaky, Irish Mick and Danny the Deathlover with him. That left him with Ethel and his boys, the ten Bristol Angels and most of his own bunch. It was a good scene if he could gain control of the situation.

He swung his hog round in a tight circle and stopped.

'OK - who's gonna ride with us?' he screamed at the top of his voice. 'When we've finished with this holiday camp, it's gonna look like the camp on Blood Island.'

Without waiting to see who was following, he accelerated away with a squeal from the rear wheel and a shower of grit from the car park. Ethel pulled away a second or two behind him and rode level.

'Here's your big chance Chop,' he shouted, and gave a knowing wink.

Chopper grinned back. Ethel understood perfectly. He flicked a glance over his shoulder. The rest of the riders were already beginning to follow.

The mob screamed down the car park and turned on to the main path. There were a couple of large signs on the path.

'No Motor Vehicles Allowed.'

Chopper weaved the hog between the signs and continued down the pedestrian walkway. Behind him, everyone followed suit.

The bikes roared along the narrow paths, scattering pedestrians like chaff. In between the lines of tightly packed chalets the mob roared, taking blind corners with the vicious squeal of rubber against tarmac, and blasting their horns to clear a path in front.

Everywhere around, people were panicking. They didn't know what was going on and they didn't like what they could see. In their blind panic to escape the marauding cyclists, they threw themselves off the paths into flowerbeds and corners of comparative safety.

The mob raced up through the chalet lines towards the centre of the camp. People had already heard them coming, and the place was almost deserted and most people sought shelter.

They passed the outdoor swimming pool, Chopper circled round it two or three times, accelerating all the time. When he tired of this, he ran the hog over a couple of ornamental flowerbeds and brought the machine to a halt.

A scream of laughter attracted his attention.

Grass, looking quite insane with the excitement, had climbed off his hog and was stripping off his trousers and boots.

With a wild scream, he bounded across the path, headed

straight for the pool and dived in.

It was a good cue. Twenty more Angels jumped, dived and dive-bombed into the pool, splashing and playing about in the water like little children. Then, soaking wet and panting for breath, they climbed out against, remounted their hogs and carved wheel patterns in the flowerbeds.

Chopper was exhilarated with the atmosphere of sheer devilry in the air.

'Hey - let's all go to the fun-fair,' he screamed.

He pointed across the camp to where the Big Wheel described slow and graceful revolutions in the sky.

The mob followed him now without question. He had shown his powers of leadership, and Big M was forgotten.

The Angels parked their bikes against the wire safety fence which surrounded the funfair and poured in through the turnstile.

Chopper made a dive for the Dodgem car track, which had just finished a ride. He ran across the floor and climbed into one of the cars, forcing children out of the way roughly. The operator responded by shutting off the power and getting the hell out of it.

Ethel ran into the control box and pulled the switch himself. As the cars sparked into life, he ran across the floor with a whoop and jumped into one himself.

'Can't do this with a hog,' shouted Chopper with a crazy laugh as he swung the Dodgem car against the side of Ethel's.

The cars thumped and crashed together until the Angels were tired of the ride. Following some invisible signals, they all aimed the cars at one side of the track and drove in a mass straight into the safety buffers. The springs and rubber dampers on the wooden construction couldn't take the concerted shock. With a splintering crash, the barrier gave way, and several of the cars broke through to crash down outside.

No one was injured, although a couple of Angels climbed out of wrecked cars and walked to their hogs with noticeable limps.

All around them there was pandemonium. Women screamed, parents rushed around trying to find their children, scoop them up and run to safety. Within minutes the funfair was empty but for the Angels.

It was no longer fun. There was nobody to impress.

Chopper led the way back to the hogs and tried desperately to think of something else to do. He looked around the camp hopefully.

There, on the skyline, he saw it. The overhead cable-car. It was still operating, carrying passengers high above the camp from one end to the other. Chopper looked up and saw pale blobs of faces peering down in wonderment at the scene below them.

'Follow me,' he shouted, and raced off across the camp towards one of the control buildings.

The three men in charge of the cable car stood blocking the entrance. One of them held a huge spanner in his hand menacingly.

'Now you bastards stay clear of here,' he shouted as the riders dismounted and approached. 'This is dangerous...there are children up there.'

The Angels closed in slowly, weighing up the situation. The three men were big and tough looking, and no-one wanted to get a crack across the skull from that spanner.

Chopper glanced behind him and saw that his followers were dubious. Fun was one thing, but even an Angel though twice about getting hurt.

'Rush 'em,' shouted Chopper. 'There's only three of them and forty of us.'

Hoping that they would follow him, he dived forward towards the spanner-wielder. He ducked and twisted cleverly as the man brought the heavy tool crashing down towards his head. The blow glanced off the side of the helmet and Chopper's impetus took the big man off his feet.

Before his friends could come to his aid, the rest of the Angels had surrounded them, with fists, chains and boots flying. It was over in a few seconds. The three men lay groaning on the floor and the Angels had control of the cable car.

Chopper seized the control handle.

'This ought to shake the bastards up a bit,' he yelled with an insane laugh, and swung the handle sharply to the 'Halt' position. The huge steel cables bearing the cars squealed violently with the sudden shock. The cars, travelling along the moving cable, rocked violently and dangerously.

Chopper pulled the control handle back again at just the right second. As the rocking cars reached the apex of their swing, the surge of power snapped through the cable making them swing back the opposite way in a vicious arc. The vibrations travelled from the cars, along the cable and made the thick steel pylons hum.

'Here - let's have a go,' shouted Ethel with a laugh and snatched the control handle from Chopper's grasp. He repeated the experiment, doing it quickly three times in a row.

Chopper looked up to see the effect. Every car on the cable was swinging and rocking violently. He could hear the frightened screams as people feared for their very lives.

There, fifty feet or more above the ground, were people who were really being blown by the Hells Angels, thought Chopper with a surge of pride. What a mind-snapper this was!

In the cars, children screamed and cried with fear as their flimsy vehicles swung crazily in the sky. Women fainted from sheer terror, even brave men wondered whether their life insurances were paid up to date.

The more religious of the passengers prayed.

Chopper took over again from Ethel, and swung the handle over to the 'Go' position. Above him, the cable ground slowly to a complete halt as the power was cut off.

Chopper ran outside and looked out across the camp. Neon signs had gone out; the fairground was as still as death. Someone had cut off the entire power supply to the camp.

'I guess it's time to go,' he said to Ethel, who nodded in agreement.

'Yeah - the fuzz ought to be well on the way here by now,' he pointed out.

Following their lead, the Angel mob returned to the parked bikes and headed for the exit. Chopper pulled up beside an overflowing litter bin and pulled out a couple of empty coke bottles.

'I'll teach the bastards to shut the power off on us,' he said, and hurled both bottles towards the nearest plate glass window. The glass shattered with a crash, and splinters showered down the side of the wall with a musical tinkle.

It was the cue for an orgy of destruction. Yelling and

screaming, the other Angels picked up every and any heavy object they could lay their hands on. Bottles, stones and flowerpots were hurled through windows and against doors. Two Angels ran across to a telephone box and ripped out the receiver and wiring. Others turned their attention to turning over litter bins, scattering the contents across the paths.

Chopper was in a dream, carried out of the world of reality by the intensity of his destructive urge. He was only dimly aware of Big M roaring up on his hog and screaming at the mob.

'Come on - let's get the hell out of here. The fuzz are coming,' he shouted nervously.

'Yeah, come on, man, it's time to move,' Ethel agreed, pulling at Chopper's arm.

Chopper snapped out of his dream. He could hear the wail of the police sirens in the distance, quickly closing in.

His mind snapped back into gear. Quickly, he looked out around the holiday camp and thought carefully.

'It's OK,' he said suddenly to Marty. 'The bastards can't touch us.'

Marty looked at him nervously.

'What do you mean, you crazy bastard,' he snapped. 'They're here.'

The police cars were very close now.

Chopper pointed right across the camp.

'Look over there,' he said. 'Fields...empty fields.'

Big M followed his pointed finger. 'So what?'

'So we go out there,' said Chopper triumphantly. 'The fuzz can't bring their cars in here - the paths aren't wide enough. They'll have to park in the car park and come after us on foot. We go out over there, and scramble the hogs across the fields until we find a way out onto the road.'

Ethel slapped him on the back.

'Hey man, I think he's right,' he said to Big M.

'It's worth a try,' snapped Marty quickly. 'We've sure got a hell of a problem on our hands if they catch us.'

He swung his Harley round and pulled back the throttle.

Just before pulling away, he turned in the saddle to look at Chopper. His eyes were cold and menacing.

'When we get back I'm going to tear you apart for this,

Chopper.' he threatened. 'I didn't want any of this...but you must have been crazy to start all this damage.'

Chopper sensed the moment of truth, and jumped in feet first.

'Bollocks,' he spat at Marty's face. Then, turning to the riders behind him; 'It was fun, wasn't it, fellers? A real piece of action, not a bloody kid's day out at the seaside?'

The roar of approval and assent behind him sounded like music in his ears. The look of undiluted hate in Marty's eyes thrilled him deep inside.

'OK, let's go,' shouted Marty and gunned the Harley into life.

The hogs roared across the camp along the narrow paths. Two coppers stood in the way bravely with their hands held stupidly in the air. When the hogs screamed down upon them, they changed their minds rapidly and threw themselves out of the way to fall into a clump of bushes.

Chopper led the group now. It was his escape route and he was in charge of the exodus. He came to the outskirts of the camp, throttled back and slewed the bike on to the grass of the sports field. He cruised across the grass, heading for the wire fence which seemed to surround the camp. His eyes flicked up and down rapidly, as he surveyed the vast expanse of wire. At last, he saw what he was looking for; a small metal gate which led out to the freedom of the fields.

He roared up to it and jumped off the hog to inspect the padlock. He looked briefly at the small and flimsy look and smiled. Running back to the hog, he quickly pulled out a tyre lever from the toolbox and set about tackling the gate. He jammed the lever through the padlock and twisted. With a sudden snap, the lock gave way under the strain.

Chopper threw open the gate and delivered an exaggerated bow to the waiting Angels.

'Gentlemen...the way out,' he said with a smirk.

When the last rider had driven through the gates, Big M decided it was time to re-assert his leadership. He glanced back across the sports field to the holiday camp. The first of the pursuing policemen had reached the edge of the field and was running towards them. Behind him, several others stood in a huddle, waiting for further orders.

'We ain't got no time to fuck about,' shouted Big M. 'It's gonna be everybody for himself, from the looks of things. Get the hell out of this town the best way you can and we'll meet up later at the Knight's Rest.'

Everyone nodded knowingly. The Knight's Rest was a transport cafe and overnight hotel for lorry drivers on the A39. The Angels had passed it on the way down and picked it out as a good meeting place in case of trouble.

'One last thing,' yelled Big M as he prepared to make his way across the fields in front of them. 'Split up as much as possible, try to keep to groups of not more than three, and I don't have to warn you to keep your mouths shut if you get nicked.'

With that, Marty took off, motioning to Freaky and Danny the Deathlover to go with him. It was a direct snub to Chopper for everyone's benefit.

Chopper smirked at Marty's departing back. Ethel slapped him on the back.

'Come on, let's ride,' he muttered with a friendly grin.

Chopper smiled back and raised one thumb in a victory sign.

'Bring Grass along,' he said. 'He makes me feel nice and safe.'

Ethel nodded over Chopper's shoulder to where Grass sat waiting on his hog beside him. Chopper nodded happily; the three of them would make a nice, tight unit. Since he was no longer saddled with Samantha, and neither Ethel nor Grass were carrying pillion passengers, they could make better time across the rough country ahead, and he respected the riding skills of both companions. Added to that, Grass was a handy man to have around in case of trouble.

The rest of the Angels sorted themselves out into small groups and started out across the bumpy field. Within a minute or so, the mass of riders was dispersed into scattered twos and threes across the countryside.

Chopper and Ethel rode side by side, with Grass tailing a few yards behind. The country was wild and uncultivated - probably owned by the holiday camp with an eye for expansion in the future, thought Chopper. The trio rode in silence for several minutes, concentrating on avoiding potholes and obstacles half-hidden in the grass.

The going was slow, but with every yard gained Chopper felt more confident and relieved. The fuzz had by now given up any thoughts of pursuit and headed back to their cars. No doubt they would try to head off as many Angels as they could on the main roads. For that reason alone, Chopper wanted to get as far across country via the fields as possible.

Chopper heard Ethel shouting to him above the sound of the hogs. He glanced across. Ethel was pointing over to the right-hand side of the field they were crossing. In the distance, Chopper could discern a line of high, straight hedges and the tops of a few scattered dwellings. It probably signified a road, or a narrow country lane.

Chopper held up his hand high in the air and slewed his hog to a halt.

'What do you think, Chop?' asked Ethel, pulling up beside him.

Chopper sucked at his teeth reflectively.

'Reckon the fuzz might just be sitting there waiting for us,' he said at length.

Ethel nodded in agreement.

'Yeah. It could well be,' he uttered thoughtfully. 'So what do you suggest?'

Chopper stared out across the countryside once more. To the left there was no sign of life before a small group of hills cut off any further view.

'How do you fancy our chances up those?' he asked, pointing.

Ethel looked, appraising the hills.

'It's hard to tell how steep they are from here,' he mused. 'But I'm willing to bet there's another road on the other side of 'em.'

'Yeah - that's what I figured,' agreed Chopper. 'So what do you think?'

Ethel considered for a few seconds.

'Would you tackle those hills if you were an ordinary motorcyclist?' he asked.

Chopper laughed. 'Not on your bloody life,' he said.

'Then there's your answer,' said Ethel with a shrug. 'We're Angels.'

The trio turned towards the hills and headed towards a five-barred gate which led into the next field.

The gate was securely padlocked. Chopper dismounted to inspect it. He took one look at the massive steel shank of the lock and realised that his tyre lever would be of no use to him this time.

'Hey - come and give us a hand,' he called to Ethel and Grass. They ran over quickly.

'We'll have to lift it off its hinges,' Chopper explained, taking a firm grip on the solid wooden frame of the gate. Ethel grabbed hold of the bottom bar and heaved. The heavy gate lifted a fraction of an inch, but refused to budge any further.

'Here, give us room to get a grip,' muttered Grass, who had watched their efforts with mild amusement. Roughly shouldering Chopper out of the way, he bent down and slid his huge, ham-like hands beneath the gate. He grunted with the exertion as he heaved the gate upwards. His thick legs trembled, and the biceps on his arms swelled like melons.

Chopper and Ethel strained with renewed effort. With a squeak from the rusty pivots, the gate lifted clear of the hinges and sagged drunkenly. Grass put his boot against one corner and pushed hard. The gate tottered for a second and crashed to the ground.

'Grass used to lift weights,' explained Ethel with a sheepish grin. Grass smiled stupidly, feeling exalted at his opportunity to show off his superior strength.

They returned to their hogs and rode through the gate into a field of swaying wheat. Almost ready for harvesting, the corn husks were a good five feet high. Chopper looked across the field towards the hedge on the far side. He set his eyes on a gap and pointed the hog in a straight line towards it.

'We'll have to go straight across,' he said, pointing.

Ethel nodded. 'I'll follow you,' he said graciously.

Chopper inched the bike into the wheat and started to push through the maze of tall stalks. The wheat flattened under his front wheel as he carved a path through it. Behind him, Ethel and Grass followed closely in his tyre tracks.

Chopper's sense of direction was good. When they finally emerged from the straw coloured jungle on the other side of the field, the gate was only a few yards away. Beyond it, cows grazed contentedly in one large pasture, then there was a patch of freshly-ploughed land before the foot of the first hill.

Two gates later, they were through to the bottom of the hills and three dozen cows were marauding through a field of ripe wheat.

Ethel cruised along the bottom of the hill, seeking the best place to climb. At last he found a narrow footpath beaten through the grass.

'We'll have to go up here,' he said to Chopper, who had already conducted his own survey.

Chopper looked up the narrow, winding path dubiously.

'It's gonna be tough,' he observed.

The pathway was steep, and loose shale complicated matters even further.

They whirled round at the sound of Grass's engine gunning up. From about ten yards away, Grass raced at the hill with his throttle wide open. The hog screamed up the first part of the slope, with the back wheel sending showers of small stones spraying out behind it. Half-way up, the rear wheel slipped sideways and the machine slewed to the gowned, slithering back down the slope without its rider.

Grass picked himself up ruefully and dusted down his jeans.

'Ain't gonna make it like that, that's for sure,' he grunted irritably.

'We'll have to walk the hogs up,' said Chopper, dismounting. He slipped the hog into first gear, holding the clutch in tightly. Then, walking alongside, he eased the clutch in gently and the bike started to inch its way up the hill.

Several times the rear wheel started to slip, and threatened to slide over on top of him, but gradually Chopper eased his machine nearer and nearer to the summit. At last he made it, and called back down to Ethel and Grass, who had been waiting expectantly.

'Right, come on up,' he yelled. 'We're back to civilisation.'

Ten minutes later, bearing assorted scratches and bruises, Ethel and Grass finally joined him. Below, just beyond the foot of the hill, lay a winding country lane.

'Well, at least going down ought to be easier than coming up,' said Chopper with a devilish grin, and plunged the bike down the side of the hill.

As the three hogs raced down the hill, an astonished farm labourer looked up from tinkering with a tractor and waved his fist at them.

Chopper and Ethel stuck two fingers up at him, cut across a field of Brussels sprouts and made their way to the gate.

Seconds later, they were racing through the narrow, winding lane at breakneck speed. They rode for several miles before Chopper spied a signpost and threw up his hands in a signal to stop. The hogs screamed to a halt leaving tyre tracks in the roadway.

'Better figure out where the hell we are,' Chopper observed, wheeling his hog round and cruising over to the signpost. It wasn't much help, only serving to inform that the village of Wootton Courtney was half a mile ahead.

'Don't look like we've got much choice,' said Ethel philosophically. They continued on down the road until they hit the village.

From there, it was much easier. Most of the main roads were signposted from the village centre, and Chopper drew on his limited knowledge of the Somerset countryside to work out a route.

To avoid the still-present threat of fuzz interception, they decided to loop down through the secondary roads, to join the A39 at Williton. From there it was a straight run of about 14 miles to Knight's Rest.

A dozen hogs were parked outside when they arrived. Inside the cafe, Chopper glanced around and saw the boys grouped around a pinball machine. There was no sign of Big M or Danny the Deathlover. Most of the riders were the Bristol Angels - who had stood the best chance of all with their greater knowledge of the district.

They greeted the new arrivals with a chorus of cheers

and laughter.

Chopper, Ethel and Grass ordered a meal and sat down to wait.

For the next hour, small groups of Angels drifted in, each new arrival being greeted with the same joyous welcome. Some twenty Angels were sitting around the transport cafe when Big M finally walked in. Chopper jumped up from his seat to greet him.

'Thought you were never coming,' he said sarcastically. Marty shoot him a look of pure undiluted hatred.

'They got Danny,' he muttered accusingly. 'The bastards were waiting for us when we hit the main road.'

Elaine smile warmly at Chopper.

'Guess we ought to thank Chopper for getting most of us out of that mess,' she said in a loud voice. A babble of muttered 'thank yous' rippled round the assembled group.

Big M flashed an evil look at her.

'Don't anyone forget that he got us into it in the first place,' he accused.

Samantha had come in with Freaky.

'Come on Big M,' she interrupted brightly, giving him a slap on the back. 'Be cool, Man...it wasn't Chopper's fault that the fuzz came chasing.'

'Yes - no sense in arguing about it now,' added Elaine. 'It's tough luck about Danny, but I reckon he'll be all right.'

Marty cast one more baleful look in Chopper's direction, then let the matter drop. He walked to the counter to order some food and cups of tea. Afterwards, he returned to the group clustered round the tables and sat down. Samantha abandoned Freaky and slid next to Chopper.

'I reckon you'd better play things pretty cool, too,' she whispered. 'Marty's been in a pretty foul temper over the way you took off.'

'It'll sort out,' said Chopper confidently. 'Things usually do.'

'Yeah,' Sammy agreed, and fell silent.

Chopper looked at the Angels sitting around the cafe. They were all unusually quiet, and restrained. At one table, a small group exchanged dirty jokes and occasionally burst into ribald laughter, but for the most part there was a sullen silence. The atmosphere was bad. The close call with the fuzz had robbed most of them of their high spirits.

Another three-quarters of an hour passed. Chopper glanced at his watch. It was seven-thirty. A few more stragglers came in, sensed the uneasy atmosphere and sat down quietly. At eight o'clock, Big M stood up and addressed the assembled company.

'Looks like everybody who's going to make it is here,' he stated flatly. There was a general murmur of assent.

Chopper made a count of heads. There were thirty two Angels and twenty four birds. The rest he assumed had either been picked up by the fuzz or had got lost and were making their own way straight back to London.

Those who remained stared at Big M impassively, expectantly. They waited for him to give the call to action which seemed as though it would never come.

Chopper jumped to his feet impulsively. The deadness of the atmosphere all around him threatened to choke everybody. A blur of faces swivelled towards him, then back to Marty. For a split second, Chopper imagined that he had been outcast like a leper, then, gradually, the faces once more turned towards him with a silent plea.

'Hey, Marty,' Chopper called loudly across the cafe. 'What say we blast out of here and get some drink inside us?'

The silence broke at last. A hurried scraping of chair legs against the floor greeted his words. A babble of conversation broke out and some of the birds giggled nervously. A warm breeze of relief swept across the cafe as the tension subsided, and new hopes flared up beneath the general depression.

Chopper had been cool - he had handed the opportunity to Marty on a golden plate, yet the initiative remained his. More important, every single person in the cafe realised it. He stared fixedly at Marty, who stood glowering at him with undisguised animosity. Marty felt trapped, restrained, unable to move one way or the another. As the precious seconds passed, he was aware of a sea of questioning faces and the mounting pressure which threatened to swamp his remaining degree of control.

It was Elaine who snapped the tension between them. Grabbing Marty's hand, she pulled him into movement, catching him off balance both physically and mentally and dragging him towards the door.

'Come on, Big M,' she whispered quietly. 'Let's get the hell out of here.'

Perhaps Marty might have chosen that very moment to make his stand, grasp with both hands what remained of his dwindling authority. Perhaps...Chopper would never know. Caught off balance, and further confused by the intervention of a mere female, Big M stumbled towards the door and the Angel horde swept to its feet joyously to follow him.

Elated, Chopper followed the main throng, sliding his arm possessively around Samantha's waist as he moved towards the exit.

Outside, the daylight was just beginning to fade and most of the day's heavy traffic had eased off, leaving the roads comparatively clear.

Night was coming - the natural habitat of the Hells Angels - the sense of freedom was once again in the air, and all was well with the small world in which they lived.

The hogs peeled away from the car park, circling aimlessly until someone gave them direction.

Big M, his composure regained, thrust the Harley through the ranks to the front position. He lifted his arm and pointed down the road toward home.

'First pub we see on the left-hand side,' he shouted, and screamed out into the road without checking for traffic.

Chopper glanced sideways as Samantha slid on to the pillion seat behind him and clasped him firmly around the waist. Freaky's eyes greeted his coldly, an unmistakable jealousy smouldering in them as Sammy pressed up closer to Chopper, her full breasts squashing softly against his back.

The fact registered dimly in the back of Chopper's mind, and was assessed into the general balance of things. Samantha was unimportant...a mere cypher in the game, yet her presence affected the relationships between individuals and would have some eventual bearing on the outcome of events.

Chopper realised that when the time came, he and Freaky would be fighting on opposite sides.

The thought rankled for a moment, then passed. Freaky, like any other individual, was expendable.

Chopper shoved the hog into gear and let out the clutch fiercely. He was still staring sideways at Freaky as the hog spurted forwards. Both knew that the time for individual friendships and enmities was past. It was time to choose sides, time to prepare for the important war-game which lay, inevitably, ahead.

The first pub turned out to be only half a mile up the road. It lay, quietly and innocently tucked back a few yards from the road as though hoping the Angels would pass it by.

They didn't. Already two dozen hogs cluttered up the small and tidy forecourt and the first invaders crossed the threshold of the quiet country pub. Once inside, they looked like aliens from another planet. Against a sombre background of creosoted wooden beams, smoke-browned white plaster and gleaming horse brasses, the figures of the Angels jarred like a whore at a wedding.

They swept in, filling the tiny lounge bar to bursting point and clustered at the bar. The publican eyed them apprehensively, sensing their basic hostility and withdrawing from it.

As he reluctantly pulled pints and dealt with the rush of orders, his eyes flashed apologetically towards the other customers. Most of them climbed reluctantly to their feet, draining their drinks and mumbling farewells as they deserted him. A couple remained, avoiding the piercing, antagonistic stares of the new arrivals by gazing sheepishly down into their half-empty glasses.

As the Angels got their drinks and moved away from the bar, the publican seemed to relax slightly. His unwanted customers seemed to be paying for what they wanted, and were offering no direct threats of violence. Perhaps he could relax, he thought. Perhaps the stories he had heard about these wild young motor-cyclists were exaggerated, unfounded. He forced these optimistic thoughts into the upper surface of his consciousness as he continued to pull away at the beer-pumps, keeping up with the demands of the thirsty horde.

As fast as he finished one order, there was another waiting to be filled. The Angels drank quickly, greedily, not wanting to waste a second before the glorious, powerful and heady feeling of drunkenness arrived to lift them into a higher state of being.

Chopper drained two pints of bitter in quick succession, ordered a third and handed Samantha a pint of light ale. Motioning her to stay close behind him, he pushed his way across the overcrowded bar to where Ethel and Trucker were holding a pint-drinking contest.

Trucker emptied the pint down his throat in a single throw, slammed the glass down on the table while Ethel was still struggling to swallow the last quarter pint. They both grinned stupidly and good-naturedly, wiping their mouths with the backs of their hands and flicking off the drops of beer which had dribbled down on to their originals. As both contestants stood puffing and trying to regain lost breath, Grass arrived with another handful of pints to replenish their losses.

Chopper accepted one gratefully quickly finishing the one he had in hand.

'Wanna try?' asked Trucker, gesturing to the full glass. Chopper grinned and shook his head.

'I wouldn't have a chance,' he admitted honestly. Trucker laughed and demolished his new drink in eight seconds flat.

Ripples of laughter ran around the pub. Girls giggled happily as Angels performed tricks to impress them, and Chopper noted that the atmosphere had turned full circle from that in the transport cafe only half an hour earlier.

He looked across to where Marty stood, Elaine by his side. He seemed more relaxed now, as he was gradually swallowed by the air of frivolity and the drink took its inevitable effect on him. Elaine was plying him with drink, encouraging him to make frequent trips to the bar and nudging him to finish when his glass was half-empty. She caught Chopper's eye and smiled knowingly. Chopper grinned back. She may as well have called to him across the room and above the din. He felt the same telepathic signal he had sensed before, when they had all turned on together in his room. Elaine was his, both by wish and by rights, and she was waiting for him to stand up and claim her.

He turned quickly from her gaze, not wishing to clash eyes with Marty. Sliding his arm round Samantha's shoulders, he clasped one breast in his fist and squeezed it tightly. The gesture was for Elaine, just as she had stripped and displayed her body for him.

'Out of the fuckin' way,' shouted a harsh voice, and all faces turned to stare at Grass, as he jostled his way through the crowds towards the bar.

He held a tall pile of pint mugs in his hand, one balanced upon another in a crazy, precarious tower. As he moved slowly towards the bar, other Angels joined in the fun and eager hands reached out to deposit yet more mugs on top of the pile. There were ten pint glasses in his hands when a bird with a sense of humour reached out and tickled him under the armpit with one sharp fingernail. Grass screamed and jumped. The pile tilted, tottered and fell to the floor in a crash of splintering glass. Everyone laughed uproariously - most of all Grass himself.

The publican was not amused. His broad, country accent cut through the noise and laughter like a wood saw.

'One more trick like that and you'll all be thrown out,' shouted the publican threateningly. His voice was harsh and uncompromising.

The laughter died a sudden death as all faces turned towards the bar. Grass starred at the publican stupidly in disbelief.

'I mean it,' the publican added. 'I'll not have any bloody yobbos in here acting like pigs.'

Grass turned back to the Angels for support. This was a direct challenge. Ethel and Trucker moved up slowly beside him. A ripple of expectancy ran through the pub, and the few remaining citizens hurriedly downed their drinks and made a discreet exit.

Chopper's eyes were fixed on Marty. He wanted to see how Big M would react to this new threat. His lips curled in a sneer as he saw the obvious discomfort on Marty's face.

The Bristol boys had meanwhile gathered around Grass. Ethel, Trucker, Frenchie and Sam the Spick stood in a line, facing the bar defiantly. The pub was ominously silent as everyone waited for action to explode at any second.

Grass reached out slowly and deliberately and picked up a pint glass off a nearby table. He held it up between finger and thumb, raised it slowly above his head and held it there. The publican stood stock still, just watching, waiting.

Perhaps half a minute passed, with the entire group poised like a tableau of mime artists. There was a complete silence.

When Grass released his grip on the mug, it seemed to float towards the cobbled stone floor in slow-motion. The crash of breaking glass sounded ten times as loud as it need be.

Still nobody moved. The publican continued to stare fixedly at Grass, who met his gaze with an even, calm stare. Then, suddenly, he swivelled on one heel and disappeared from behind the bar without a word.

Grass relaxed. As far as he was concerned, a moral victory had been gained.

Big M's voice cut across the silent pub.

'OK - let's drink up and get going. He's gone to phone the fuzz.'

Marty got to his feet and dragged Elaine up with him. Downing the remainder of his pint, he slammed the glass down upon the table and started to move towards the door. Grass pivoted round to confront him.

'What the fuck are you doing, Man?' he asked incredulously. 'You mean we're just going to quietly up and sneak out like naughty kids?'

Marty stared at him with a cool, level gaze.

'You got a better idea?'

Grass snorted in disgust.

'You bet I got a better idea,' he said. 'I reckon we ought to teach this little bastard a little lesson. Nobody fucks around with the Angels and gets away with it.'

To add emphasis to his words, he picked up another glass and hurled it towards the tow of optics above the bar. Two bottles shattered, and whisky splashed down over the counter into an amber puddle.

Sam the Spick lifted up a table and overturned it. Half-full glasses of beer fell to the floor and smashed.

Marty continued walking towards the door.

'Anyone who wants to spend the night in the nick can stay here,' he called over his shoulder. 'Otherwise I suggest you follow me.'

Chopper's lips curled into a sneer as he looked at Big M in disgust. This was the final straw, he decided. Big M had at last made his final, fatal mistake. He waited for the seemingly inevitable clash between Grass and Marty. Most of the other Angels fidgeted nervously, wondering what to do. No-one liked the idea of walking out meekly, not when there was the opportunity for mayhem, and more than sufficient grounds for justification.

Big M's hold over the Angels might have been broken for ever at that precise moment in time, had it not been for the re-appearance of the publican behind the bar.

'I warned you,' he said quietly and menacingly. 'Now get out of here.'

The twin barrels of a twelve-bore shotgun added all the emphasis in the world to his words. It was pointed at Grass's legs.

'Get out,' repeated the publican coldly. 'Before my finger has accident with this trigger.'

Grass stared at the twin muzzles of death in fascination.

'You wouldn't dare,' he said defiantly, but his voice had a tremor in it.

The publican smiled grimly.

'Maybe not,' he agreed, 'But do you want to be a cripple for the rest of your life just to make sure?'

Everyone standing within six feet of Grass shuffled away as though he had leprosy. They were well aware of the scatter effect of a shotgun.

Grass shifted uncertainly on his feet. He was certain that the man was bluffing...yet there was always the chance...

His hand edged out slowly and rested on the nearest table. His fingers crawled across the table top until they encountered a glass. Without moving his eyes from the shotgun for a second, he lifted it, with infinite slowness, into the air.

The publican's face was stiff and immobile. Beads of sweat had broken out on his forehead and were trickling down the side of his nose. He shifted the gun almost imperceptibly to follow Grass's arm as it drew back gradually into a throwing position.

The tension was electrifying. Some of the girls had already begun to shiver with fear, and even the most daring of the Angels had quietly returned their glasses to tables and were beginning to back towards the door.

Chopper looked at Grass and felt a surge of admiration for his class. Yet he too feared that the publican might just fulfil his threat, and Grass could call his bluff by hurling the glass any second.

Grimly, he moved slowly towards Grass and stretched out his hand. With a sudden movement, he snatched the pint mug from his hand and placed it on the table.

'Come on, Man,' he murmured gently, patting Grass on the back. 'There's always another time.'

Grass seemed to tense up even more for a second, then his shoulders slumped with resignation. He turned slowly, and followed Chopper out of the pub.

The publican watched impassively as the Angels filed out through the door. Only when the very last motor-cycle engine had roared away and faded into the distance did he relax.

With a grim smile, he pointed the shotgun up towards the ceiling and his finger tightened on the trigger.

Savagely, he pulled it back.

The two hammers fell with a sharp click upon the empty breech.

Riding a hog and raising Hell pretty well tops the list of Hells Angels pastimes, but sex comes a pretty close second.

With the earlier excitement of the day fading into memory and material for future legend, and the drink roaring in their heads, many of the Angels were beginning to think along these lines.

Big M didn't have to be told. He knew full well that the run would not be complete without a party in the true Angel tradition.

He had been keeping his eyes open for a suitable venue since leaving the pub twenty minutes earlier, and now, in the glare of his headlights, he could see it.

A farm, up for sale. The noticeboard was plain, and explicit.

Several factors flashed through Marty's mind - all of them favourable.

A farm up for sale was extremely likely to be deserted. Farms had barns, hay-lofts and other suitable places for drinking and screwing. Both these activities were the essential ingredients for an Angel party. Farms also had the added attraction of being tucked away from main roads, and were invariably isolated. Isolation meant security from unwanted prying eyes, and unlikely places for fuzz intervention.

Big M blasted his horn by way of a signal and slewed the Harley to a halt. The others followed his lead, pulling their hogs together in a tight formation. They waited expectantly.

'OK...it's party time,' shouted Big M, and a chorus of joyous whoops greeted his announcement.

Marty summoned Freaky, Irish Mick and Screwball Sam.

'Better go get some liquor,' he said, fishing in his denim jacket for a roll of notes. He peeled off thirty quid in fivers and handed it to Freaky.

'Ditch any birds and go get some beer,' he said. 'Head up the road to the nearest pub, get the stuff and come back here. We'll be down on the farm.' He gestured back down the road to where he had seen the notice board.

Vicar, leader of the Bristol contingent, pulled up alongside Big M.

'Reckon we'll make our contribution,' he said, and flashed a thick bundle of pound notes. He summoned four of his riders, handed over the money and told them to follow Freaky.

'We'd better take more hands,' said Irish Mick, and beck-oned to three more riders to go with him. 'Fifty quid ought to buy a fair amount of booze.'

Big M grinned. 'It'd better,' he said. 'Otherwise we'll have to make another trip to Dalston.'

The joke was greeted with a guffaw of laughs. The money was from communal Angel funds - partially made up from weekly subscriptions, but the most part coming out of the pockets of skinheads after a recent fight in the Dalston area. There was little else one could do to an unconscious Skinhead than to lift his wallet.

The small beer-fetching party raced off down the road. Big M wheeled his hog round in the road and led the way back to the farm entrance.

Just as he had suspected, a long winding track led down to the farm buildings, which appeared to be completely deserted. Marty motioned the others to follow and drove carefully down the track, his headlight carving a pathway through the darkness.

Arriving at the farm buildings, the Angels inspected the premises. The door to the farmhouse was securely bolted, and large wooden planks had been nailed across the windows. The farm looked as though it had been empty for several months.

Big M cruised around the immediate area, looking for a suitable building. After a few minutes, he returned to the pack triumphantly.

'Just the place,' he announced proudly. 'There's a beautiful big barn - complete with wall to wall straw carpeting.'

He led the way down to the big barn and drove straight inside. In the glare of the hog lights, the figures of rats scur-ried about as they ran to escape from the noisy invaders.

Big M parked his hog up against one wall and switched off the engine. Switching on his parking light, he called to several other Angels to do the same.

The Angels dismounted with screams and war-cries, and flung themselves down into the straw. The setting couldn't have been more perfect for a party. Dim lights, plenty of soft straw to sit on or screw on, and soon there would be plenty of booze. Max produced a transistor radio and tuned into Radio

Luxembourg. Now they even had music.

Chopper sat down beside his hog and pulled Samantha to his side. Fishing in his pocket, he pulled out a pack of cigarette papers and the small parcel of hash he had brought with him.

'Reckon we might as well have a little smoke while we're waiting,' he said to no-one in particular, and set about rolling a couple of joints. Half-a-dozen Angels recognised the familiar pungent smell as he cooked the hash, and drifted over to his side.

It brought Elaine too.

'Smells like fun,' she murmured softly. Chopper looked up from his labour of love with some surprise.

'You want to join me?'

Elaine smiled.

'You know I'm always interested.'

The simple statement carried a wealth of double meanings. Chopper got the message plainly enough.

'Sit down,' he invited. 'As long as Lord and Master doesn't mind.'

Elaine tossed her head contemptuously.

'I don't give a shit,' she snapped.

Chopper nodded understandingly, but decided not to say anything. Instead, he busied himself finishing the joint and lighting it. Taking two deep pulls, he passed it on to Elaine. She sucked greedily at the acrid smoke and handed it on to Samantha, who took her quota and passed it on in turn.

The little group sat in silence for a few minutes, as the reefer slowly burned away and imparted its own special brand of magic. As it dwindled to a mere stub, Chopper rolled another and moved it into the circle. He was just beginning to feel good when Freaky and the boys arrived back with the drink.

Shouts and whistles of approval greeted them as they staggered into the barn, weighed down with crates of beer and bottles of wine. There was a mad scramble, as everyone rushed for the booze greedily.

'Sammy - go get me a beer,' said Chopper. Samantha got to her feet meekly.

'Sure Chopper,' she said quietly and forced herself into

the fray.

Chopper turned to Elaine, now that they were alone.

'Well?' he muttered, staring her in the eyes.

She met his gaze with calm intensity.

'You've got it pretty well tied up,' she said softly, as a faint smile played about her lips. 'All the moves are up to you.'

Chopper nodded.

'You want in?' he asked.

Elaine's eyes flashed.

'Yes, I want in,' she responded. 'But I don't come easy.'

Chopper smiled wryly.

'I didn't expect you to,' he said. Then, after a pause: 'You know there's going to be a fight?'

Elaine nodded in agreement.

'Yes,' she agreed. 'But not for the reasons you might think.'

Chopper looked at her quizzically. 'How do you mean?'

'Marty would hand over control of all the Hells Angels in the world quite happily,' she replied. 'He doesn't care any more - he's gone soft...But he knows that when he gives up the Angels, he'll be giving up me - and that's what he'll fight to protect. Marty knows how I feel about the Angels...how I feel about life.'

Chopper stared at her piercingly.

'So if I didn't want you, I could take over with no trouble?' he asked.

Elaine grinned.

'Maybe,' she murmured. 'But you do want me, don't you, Chopper?'

Chopper looked over her lithe, sensuous body.

'Yeah,' he grunted reflectively. 'You know bloody well I do.'

Elaine laughed. 'Good,' she said, 'I like a men to lust after me...it keeps my ego going. Marty wants to smother me, crush me down to a horrible, ordinary existence. He wants the full bit...marriage, half a dozen flying ducks on the wall, slippers by the fire and three snotty-nosed little bastards running around the floor. He's even got some crazy idea about running a little hog repair shop of his very own.'

'And you?' Chopper asked. 'What do you want?'

Elaine wriggled sexily.

'Me, I just like the simple pleasures in life,' she said with a smile. 'Like screwing, and drink and excitement. Kicks, Chopper - that's what life is about. Just kicks - in any shape or form.'

'You'll get as much as you can handle,' vowed Chopper sliding out one arm to grasp her round the waist.

Elaine wriggled away expertly and got to her feet.

'But first you've got to prove yourself, Chopper,' she murmured warningly. 'And like I said - it won't be easy.'

She smiled briefly and walked off back to the other side of the barn where Big M and Freaky sat throwing back beers. Chopper's eyes followed her, taking in the curve of her hips and the gentle sway of her buttocks.

'Bitch,' he swore silently under his breath. 'I'll make you crawl for it one day.'

'Here, Chop.'

Chopper glanced up, took the proffered can of beer from Samantha and stretched himself luxuriously in the straw as she lay down beside him. Her hand crept across his thigh to nestle in the warm softness of his groin, and her fingers began a gentle, stimulating massage.

He relaxed, forcing thoughts of Elaine from his mind and let Samantha's well-practised hands complete the work that the beer and hashish had started.

Samantha slid down his zipper, and deftly unclipped the press-stud at the top of his jeans, allowing the throbbing flesh relief from the constricting pressure of the rough material. Her finger nails tickled and teased, carving patterns of delicious pleasure from his thighs to his waist.

A boot prodded him impatiently in the side of the rib-cage. Chopper looked up to see Irish Mick towering above him, with a can of beer held in either hand.

'Hey - come over and watch the fun, Man,' he chuckled. 'Doreen's doing a fiver.'

Chopper glanced down at Samantha, who had now abandoned herself to her favourite sexual deviation.

'You ought to take up smoking cigars instead,' he said to her jokingly, and slid his fingers under her hair to where her chin rested on his thigh. He pulled her face away roughly and scrambled to his feet.

'Later, baby.' He zipped himself up and followed Irish
Mick, leaving Samantha to seek a new source of pleasure. She
looked around dreamily for a few seconds, shrugged and
wriggled across the straw to where one of the Bristol Angels
sat alone consoling himself with a bottle of wine.

Introductions weren't necessary. To Samantha, one Angel
was much the same as another.

Irish Mick led the way across the barn to where a dozen or so
Angels and their birds sat in a tight circle, forming an impromptu
arena. In the centre stood Doreen - the star of the show.

She had stripped off and was busy helping Screwball Sam
to do the same. Mudso and Frenchie had contented themselves with removing their jackets and unzipping their
jeans. Just two more volunteers were needed before the
show could commence.

Doreen looked around the circle of faces. Her eyes fell upon
Chopper and she grinned wickedly.

'Wanna be in on the act, Chop?' she called to him.

Chopper shook his head with a laugh.

'Not me, babe,' he said. 'But Mick here fancies a go.'

He nudged Irish Mick in the ribs, pushing him forward.
Drunkenly, Mick stumbled towards the arena pushing
through the ring of Angels with his broad chest and shoulders
whilst drinking beer with one hand and unzipping his jeans
with the other.

A tall blonde Angel from Bristol called Tex made up the five.

Screwball Sam lay down on the floor in readiness. Doreen
stood over him with her legs astride, rubbing her palm furiously under her crotch to stimulate her natural lubrication.
Then, as the Angels cheered her on, she sank slowly to her
knees over Sam's prostrate body and manoeuvred herself into
the correct position. With a soft moan of satisfaction, she sank
on to him and wriggled lasciviously. The plump cheeks of her
bottom quivered like a jelly on springs.

She bent forwards over Sam, raising her haunches in the air
for the second participant to take his advantage. Frenchie, his
jeans down around his ankles, moved into position behind her.

The strange mountain of flesh grew even more as Irish Mick

slithered forward to sit on Screwball Sam's chest. Sam grinned at the assembled onlookers.

Doreen giggled drunkenly and leaned forward until she was no longer able to make any sounds at all. To complete the bizarre scene, Mudso and Tex sat down on either side of her and guided her hands to work.

Chopper felt a tightness growing in his jeans as he watched with mounting fascination. Doreen's whole body moved and twitched furiously as she abandoned all control and was swept away on a savage tide of unnatural passion.

Chopper glanced sideways, noting the effect that the erotic scene was having on everyone watching. Next to him, a small red-headed girl stood with an Angel's arm drooped around her shoulder and his hand busily massaging her breast. One of her hands was equally busy between her own legs. Her eyes were glassy, and her breathing heavy and irregular. Chopper smiled indulgently and switched his attention back to Doreen and her famous party piece.

She was in the last throes of sexual exhaustion now. Her movements were more frantic and less co-ordinated. her breathing was desperate, as she tried to catch a lung-full of air whenever possible. From time to time she seemed to collapse from the effort of it all and lay exhausted upon Screwball Sam, only contracting her thigh muscles gently to keep the rhythm going. Suddenly, she seemed to be spurred on to a last, furious surge of movement. She twisted and writhed as if in agony for a few seconds, then flopped completely. Only Frenchie continued moving for a few seconds more then everyone was as still as death.

A chorus of cheers and scattered handclaps burst from the spectators. Freaky's excited voice broke the stunned silence.

'They're stuck together...need a bucket of water like dogs.' A ripple of drunken laughter greeted his joke.

Chopper backed away quickly, not wishing to be pulled in to the game. He looked for Samantha, saw her pumping herself up and down on top of her new friend, smiled resignedly to himself and gazed around the barn for alternative action.

Across the other side of the barn, the little blonde known as Sparky lay on her back with her legs open to the all-time gang-bang record. She had already pulled a train of five Angels, and waited impatiently for the next. Chopper slid over to oblige her.

From the corner of his eye, he spied Big M, leaning drunkenly up against one wall with a seven-pint can of beer held to his upturned mouth. There was no sign of Elaine.

Chopper finished himself with the quiescent Sparky, and rolled off her onto his back. Pausing only to zip himself up again, he stood up and went in search of beer.

As he uncapped a bottle of light ale, Big M staggered up behind him and started to rummage about in the crates for a fresh can. He picked up another large party canister and pulled out the rubber bung, loosing a thick jet of beer which spurted across the barn.

Marty raised the can to his lips unsteadily, and gulped down the beer. His eyes flicked over Chopper glassily, without recognition. Then, with a lurching, unsteady gait, he turned and staggered back to the far wall.

'He's pissed as a fart,' said Elaine's voice in disgust. She stood behind Chopper, glaring after the departing figure of her man. 'Poor little bastard is so upset he's just been drinking continuously for the past hour.' As she spoke, her lips curled into a contemptuous sneer. 'Fat lot of good he's going to be to me.'

As they both looked, Marty staggered into the wall, bounced off and fell in a drunken heap on to the floor. He clambered up to his knees groggily, gave a sudden heave and sprayed a thick stream of vomit across the room. The can of beer dropped from his hands on to his lap, where it discharged its contents over his jeans. Marty vomited again and collapsed into drunken dreams.

'See what I mean?' asked Elaine pointedly. She reached down to pick up an empty beer bottle and hurled it in Marty's direction. It missed by a few inches.

'He'll be OK in a few minutes,' muttered Chopper. 'Now that he's flashed, he'll get his second wind.'

Elaine snorted. 'Not on your bloody life,' she said vehemently. 'Once he crashes, he's out for a couple of hours. Believe me...I know.'

Chopper shrugged.

'He used to be able to out-drink anyone in the bunch - and

still stay on his feet,' he said.

'Yeah - Marty used to be able to do a lot of things muttered Elaine. 'Like I said...he's gone soft.'

Chopper cast a glance over to the sleeping figure of Big M. His very nickname seemed a joke now, he thought. There was nothing big about Marty Gresham any more. Chopper felt a surge of pity and nostalgia for the friend he had once admired and respected. Marty had introduced him to the Angels, given him a whole way of life.

Elaine seemed to read his thoughts.

'Don't pity him,' she said. 'He had a good run, I suppose.'

Chopper surveyed the party. Doreen was still naked, but seemed to have regained her vitality and was engaged in a heavy petting session with Vicar. Samantha had moved on to Freaky, who was lying on his back throwing down beer while she nuzzled happily between his legs. Grass and Ethel were still holding their eternal beer-drinking contest and Irish Mick was fighting playfully with Mudso. Sparky still lay where Chopper had left her, but since then three more Angels had taken advantage of her obliging person. The rest of the company sat and stood around drinking, rolling in the straw, urinating against the walls or singing filthy rugby songs.

'Let's take a walk,' Chopper said to Elaine, gesturing towards the barn door.

She shrugged.

'OK.'

They walked slowly towards the door, carefully stepping over bodies and pools of beer and vomit whenever necessary. No-one paid them the slightest attention, and Marty was too fast asleep to worry.

Outside, the darkness was complete. Even the quarter moon shed no real light. The night was warm, and a lazy breeze rustled through the hedges and trees.

Elaine grasped Chopper's hand as they walked away from the barn until the noise of the party was only a dim sound in the distance.

As his eyes grew accustomed to the darkness, Chopper could pick out things more clearly. The flat bulk of a large wooden building loomed up in front of them.

'Let's go in there,' said Elaine, pointing.

Chopper looked down at her face with mild astonishment. Her inviting mouth was drooping half-open, and even in the weak light he could see there was a strange sparkle in her eyes.

Gone was the former self-assurance, the certain knowledge of her own undeniable feminine charms. Elaine was no longer a beautiful, but unattainable creature. Her attitude to him had changed completely...now it was she who made all the moves, plainly proclaimed her availability.

'Come on,' she urged, pulling at Chopper's hand. They reached the building, and Elaine pulled at the heavy door.

It was open. As the door swung back, the heady smell of old hay came to Chopper's nostrils. The building had obviously been a hay-loft, or perhaps a stable. Certainly there was a smell of something more than dead grass about the place.

Elaine led him inside the door, across the straw-covered stone floor to a tall pile of hay in one corner.

'Here,' she murmured simply, as she flung herself down.

Chopper sank down beside her.

'Here? Now?' he repeated querulously. 'I thought you wanted me to prove myself first.'

Elaine chuckled deep in her throat. 'Maybe I want you to prove something else right now,' she whispered softly. 'Let me know what I'm letting myself in for. Being leader of the pack can be a pretty demanding job, Chopper. I wonder if you're up to it.'

Chopper groped in the darkness for her neck. Gripping it savagely, he twisted her face upwards to meet his.

'I'll show you what I'm up to,' he hissed, pressing Elaine down into the soft hay. His lips closed over hers in a tentative, exploratory kiss. They were warmer than he had expected. There was not the slightest trace of resistance. Elaine's arm curled around his shoulder and her sharp fingernails stroked his back gently.

Chopper poked the tip of his tongue into her half open mouth, licking slowly and gently along the underside of her full, soft top lip. Elaine squirmed sensuously and her mouth opened even wider to receive him.

Chopper thrust his tongue deep into her mouth and roved

across her teeth and tongue. The fingernails in his back lost their gentle touch and became thorns pressing into his flesh. Elaine responded by licking the edge of his lips. Chopper gripped it quickly between his teeth and bit until Elaine released a tiny squeal of pain.

Then his fingers were busy slipping under her sweater and roving in small, lazy circles over her stomach. Elaine quivered with pleasure, wriggling her behind as though to screw herself down into the hay. Chopper explored her smooth body slowly, carefully, noting every inch of her flesh and where his touch had the most effect. He smiled to himself as Elaine's excitement increased. She was a whole mass of erogenous zones, each one seeming to inflame her yet further. His fingers probed her back, noting the particularly sensitive spot between her shoulder blades, and picked at the clip of her brassiere.

Chopper undid it with a well-practised flip of his fingers and moved the palm of his hand slowly back over her shoulders and down the swelling mounds of her breasts.

They were soft yet firm, as he had so many times imagined they would be. Her nipples stood out like little buds, almost ready to burst into flower. Taking one between his finger and thumb, he squeezed it experimentally, gently at first and them more savagely.

Elaine seemed to respond to pain more than to gentle approach. Her breath rasped in his ear as he increased the pressure of his fingers.

As Chopper continued to play with her breasts, she pulled her arms free from underneath him and started to peel off her sweater. It came off over her head, and with a little shrug of her shoulders, the loose bra fell from her body.

Chopper moved to the catch of her trousers, slipping his fingers underneath the tight waistband to stroke the incredibly soft flesh of her lower belly. She unzipped herself, writhing her bottom as she struggled to ease the pants over her hips.

Chopper was taking little pleasure from this exercise. His mind was cool, free from any emotions at all, and his approach was as cold and clinical as that of a surgeon. He realised that he was on test, and he intended to pass with flying colours.

Elaine's fingers were busy removing his clothing as Chopper finally deigned to touch the very centre of her sexual being. Curling his fingers gently in the short, springy hair, he stroked gently at the outer lips, smoothed over the soft fleshy mound surrounding her hot, moist little pleasure cave and slowly massaged her erected clitoris.

Elaine moaned softly as Chopper finally, and so slowly inserted his finger. Her bottom lifted from the floor as she thrust herself upwards to meet him.

'Come on you bastard,' she whispered through gritted teeth. 'Can't you see I'm ready?'

Chopper smiled down at her with ice-cold detachment.

'Not half as ready as you're gonna be,' he muttered calmly, and sank his teeth into the full ripeness of her breasts.

Elaine muttered muffled curses at him and gyrated her hips frantically as his finger once again slid out to stroke across her throbbing clitoris.

'Fuck me, baby, fuck me,' Elaine pleaded, as she moved herself even more furiously against him. Chopper responded by deliberately slowing down his movements, but increasing the pressure.

'Say please,' he snarled at her.

Elaine screamed at him through clenched teeth.

'Please, you beautiful bastard...please.' She gave a cry of which was half laughter, half pain. The scream died as it was choked with pleasure. Her body trembled as the first wave of orgasm picked her up and carried her away.

Chopper felt the wetness of her flood hotly across his hand. Elaine's whole body was quivering as though she had a fever. Now, he thought, now I'll show her what it's all about.

He shifted his body across her, forcing her thighs apart roughly with one quick movement of his hands. Then, grasping his penis firmly in one fist, he guided it in so that just the tip entered her.

Chopper contracted his stomach muscles slowly, pulling himself carefully back until he was ready.

With Elaine's pleas ringing in his ears, Chopper lunged forward, thrusting himself inside her like a battering ram. Elaine screamed loudly with pain and pleasure and continued to groan as he pounded away until the climax arrived to drain his body of energy.

Afterwards, they lay breathless for several minutes, saying nothing.

Elaine broke the silence.

'That's the first time anyone ever did that,' she whispered softly.

'Did what?' muttered Chopper dozily.

Elaine cuddled up to his side like a soft warm kitten.

'Made me have more than one,' she said. 'I came twice.'

'I know,' said Chopper calmly. 'It would have been more, only I thought you ought to be introduced gently.'

Elaine chuckled happily.

'You big-headed bastard,' she joked. She lay quiet for a while. 'I'll tell you something else,' she said at last. 'You've just won yourself the leader's girl...all you got to do now is be the leader.'

'Soon,' said Chopper confidently. 'Very soon.'

'You might need my help.'

'Yes, I might.'

'I will help you Chopper. I'll do anything for you...now.'

The pause in her voice was like a victory war-cry in Chopper's ears. Now he knew he had won, knew that the battle had been fought and decided. Now it just a matter of timing, planning, and manoeuvring the situation to fit requirements.

'Phone me at work if you need me,' said Elaine. 'You know where I work, don't you?'

'Yeah,' said Chopper, his mind already racing off along paths of the near future.

Elaine fumbled in the darkness for her clothes.

'I guess we'd better get back,' she said.

They dressed in silence.

The lights in the old barn were plainly visible as they came out of the hay-loft. Even without them, Chopper could have homed in on the noise. The party was still going full swing a they returned and slipped in through the door as unobtrusively as they had left.

Chopper glanced over to where Marty had been. He was no longer there. Chopper looked around in consternation and saw

Marty bearing down on them from the other side of the barn. He was still roaring drunk, and his walk was unsteady.

'Where the hell have you been?' he mumbled in a slurred tone to Elaine. He purposely avoided Chopper.

'I took her outside, she was sick,' put in Chopper quickly.

'Yeah - that's right, I was feeling sick,' said Elaine in agreement. 'You'd already crashed and Chopper helped me.'

Big M stared at her accusingly, then turned to Chopper. Disbelief was plain in his eyes. Chopper stared him out, hoping that Marty was too drunk to be too inquisitive. He wasn't ready for the final showdown yet.

Help came from an unexpected quarter.

'You feeling better now love,' said a female voice. Chopper turned round quickly to see Samantha, who had been lying down just behind them. She rose and put her arm around Elaine's shoulder.

'You was looking bloody awful,' she continued. 'Flashed it all up now, have you?'

Elaine responded to the cue quickly.

'Yeah,' she said. 'I'm all right now. Jesus, but was I sick.'

She flung her arms around Marty. 'Let's go and sit down, babe. I'm still feeling a bit weak.'

Marty paused for a moment, looking stupid and trying to run facts through his befuddled mind. But Samantha's intervention had swayed the delicate balance. Marty had - at least for the time being - swallowed the story.

'OK,' he muttered thickly, and staggered away with Elaine clinging tightly to his side.

Chopper looked at Samantha. An amused smile played about her lips.

'Thanks,' he mumbled simply. 'But why?'

Sammy shrugged her shoulders.

'Fuck it...I like you,' she said, and turned on her heel and walked away.

Chopper sat down alone and relaxed. It had been a close call, but he had come through. He felt a new surge of power deep inside him - power which told him he was invincible, top of the pile. He had everything going for him, just like he wanted it to be.

Tomorrow, after a night's sleep in the barn, they would all head back to London.

Then the real planning could begin in earnest.

Chopper's brain was still going over potentials and possibilities when he fell asleep.

Marty Gresham was worried. He had too many problems to cope with. Rather, he had one big problem, with a whole lot of minor hassles attached to it.

It wasn't a situation he could punch or kick his way out of. Lying, cheating or conniving wouldn't help him either.

It was the worst sort of problem to have...one which is too abstract to be grabbed by the scruff of its neck and shaken until it resolves itself.

That was most of the trouble - there was nothing direct that he could do, nothing solid for him to sink his teeth into.

For the sixth time in two days, he phoned Elaine.

This time she was in. Ever since coming back from the run, Elaine had either been out or her telephone was out of order...or off the hook.

'Hi babe. What d'you fancy doing tonight?' he asked.

There was a long pause. Too long. Eventually Elaine spoke in a cold distant voice.

'Hello, love,' she said weakly. 'How you doing?'

Marty was relieved to hear the sound of her voice - even if it didn't sound too happy.

'OK, I guess,' he said. 'Been trying to get hold of you.'

'Yeah - been out a lot.'

There was another long, nervous pause. Finally Elaine spoke again.

'To tell you the truth, babe...I'm feeling pretty rough. You know? Flag's up, Man, and I've got these terrible stomach cramps. Y'know?'

'You wanna come out?' asked Marty, knowing the answer before he heard it.

'I don't feel like anything right now, Marty. Phone me tomorrow, hey?'

Marty's spirits sank to ground zero.

'Yeah, OK. I'll phone you tomorrow,' he repeated blankly, and hung up.

He walked across the floor of his room irritably, kicking angrily at a fallen cushion on the floor. Rage and frustration boiled up inside him. His mind raced.

Fuck it, he knew Elaine was lying. Flag day, buggered! She was on the pill and regular as clockwork. Marty had a good memory for dates and Elaine wasn't due on for another week. For a moment he considered going round and dragging her out by force.

But what was the use? She was all part of the problem...Elaine WAS the problem.

Marty struggled to find a single solid reason why her attitude to him should have changed so suddenly. Why had she gone sour on him? Why had everything suddenly gone sour?

He sat down on the edge of his bed and lit a cigarette. He'd been lighting cigarettes and sitting on his bed for two days now - and he was still no nearer sorting out the tangle of vague ideas and half-facts.

Most of the ideas were negative ones - which made things even worse.

Marty considered the facts as he saw them, and tried to fit them into a fully rational picture.

Fact 1: He was 29 years old...coming up for his thirtieth birthday. Thirty was old - even by ordinary standards. For an Angel, it seemed like retirement time.

Fact 2: The life of a Hells Angel no longer had its former kick for him. Something deep inside him was screaming to him to cool off, calm down, slow up. Even speed had lost its thrill, and in recent months had even begun to frighten him a little.

Yes...that was an important factor surely? Big M had started to feel fear, recognise the sense of danger. Recently, it seemed, he had started to value his own life, realise that he wanted to live.

But what sort of life? Was leading the miserable existence of a pig citizen called living?

Marty could call up a hundred such questions. The trouble was there were no answers.

Fact 3: Elaine. She was inextricably tied up in it all, woven into the threads of his life, both past and present. Future too. What were her true feelings? What did she want? Did she, as she had so often explained to him, want to spend the rest of her life seeking the next thrill, the next kick?

...And what was wrong with getting married, raising a couple of kids and still trying to live outside the tiny and narrow world of the citizen?

Marty knew that he was losing the respect of his fellow riders. Only friendship remained - and a degree of loyalty which made up a big part of the Angel code. But loyalty was not enough. Not when there was someone else around who was offering them the wildness and sheer excitement in life that he had once offered.

Fact 4: Chopper. His best and closest friend, trusted follower. Now Chopper openly despised him and made no pretences about his contempt. Chopper had become a Hells Angel under Marty's persuasive guidance. He had accepted and honoured Angel traditions, embraced the way of life as though he was born to it. Now he was a true Angel - perhaps more so than his teacher had ever been. Chopper was younger, still had more of the animal wildness in him. More than that, he had the urge to be on top inside him...and Marty knew how strong that urge could be.

...And those, briefly, were the facts which Marty had to juggle with and manipulate until they fell into some sort of coherent pattern. He could easily hand over control of the Angels to Chopper. The boys would accept him happily - the events of the previous weekend showed that. But what of Elaine? How would she react to a deposed leader? When Big M ceased to be Big M and became plain Marty Gresham, would she stick with him?

...Or would she want to move on to the next top man?

Elaine: Chopper: Marty struggled with a niggling suspicion buried deep in his brain. That night...Chopper and Elaine coming in from the outside. A weak excuse...Elaine acting strangely and refusing to make love. Her attitude to him ever since...her excuses now.

Marty dredged the suspicion up, tried to wipe the cobwebs from it and fitted it into his pattern of thought.

Suddenly it wasn't a mere suspicion any more...it was a cold, hard fact.

It fitted in with the pieces and started to make a pattern. An ugly, nauseating pattern.

Marty's stomach contracted as he tried to control the fierce surge of anger which welled up inside him. He failed.

Crossing the room quickly, he threw on his riding clothes and loaded up with essential armaments. First he would go round to see Elaine, and if necessary, beat the truth out of her.

...And then Chopper, for the showdown which just had to come.

One way or another, Big M was going to prove something tonight.

While Marty Gresham was sorting out his problems, Chopper has also been going over the same facts in his mind, but from a slightly different angle. So far, he had manipulated the fates exactly how he wanted. The rest needed careful planning.

The events of the weekend had taught him many things. For the first time he could see his final goal clearly and he knew where help was likely to be found.

He made a mental count of his potential allies and enemies.

The majority of the Angels would be on his side, he felt sure...provided he didn't transgress any of the strict codes along the way. Elaine would be a useful friend to have if any undercover work was needed. There was no-one closer to Marty.

Danny the Deathlover could probably be counted as a direct enemy now, Chopper reflected bitterly. He was annoyed about that - Danny was a good Angel, and they had been good friends.

Although he had managed to escape criminal charges after his arrest back at the holiday camp, Danny was not pleased about the tight scrape he had been in...and he blamed Chopper for bringing it about. Freaky would also be likely to stand against him - mainly for personal reasons. Max usually went along with Freaky, and Irish Mick was a dubious quality altogether. He would probably swing along with whoever got to him first.

Ethel and his boys were useful, but could have no direct effect upon changes taking place in a different chapter.

Chopper mused upon these thoughts, finally coming to the conclusion that he was out on his own for the time being. It was not a healthy feeling.

Chopper needed more assistance...but from which quarter?

He racked his brains for an answer. At last, it came to him in a flash of inspiration, and he wondered why he hadn't thought of it before.

Mike Garman and his little mob of Greasers! Who better to help him...given the right incentives.

And Chopper knew just what those incentives were.

He planned and plotted carefully, making sure he had left no angle uncovered. At last, he was ready to put the final moves into operation.

Chopper knew where to find Mike Garman and his bunch.

There was no time like the present. He dressed hurriedly, and set out on the final stage of his scheme.

The Greasers always hung out in 'The Duke of Argyle' - a scruffy pub in Dalston. It wasn't the safest places for a lonesome Hells Angel to go wandering, but Chopper had no choice but to take the risk.

The pub was packed as Chopper walked in. On a small stage, a pathetic rock group banged out the bilge they passed off as music, and kids of varying ages stood around drinking and chatting up birds. Skinheads weren't much in evidence, and those who were around looked a pretty weedy bunch. Chopper felt relieved as he assessed the situation.

Garman was there, as Chopper had been hoping. Surrounded by several of his cronies, he lounged against the wall just outside the ladies toilet, touching up little girls as they came out.

Chopper walked up to the bar and ordered a pint of bitter. He waited for Garman to spot him. Chopper's originals made him stand out in the crowded pub.

He didn't have to wait long.

'Hello there, Chopper,' snivelled Garman, patting him on the back as though they were the greatest of old friends. He glanced furtively around to see if his friends were suitably impressed. Chopper repressed the sneer of disgust which threatened to come over his face.

Instead, he forced an ingratiating smile.

'Hi, Mike. How goes things?' he said heartily. Garman visibly expanded with pride.

'Pretty good, Man, pretty good,' he said loudly. 'Hear you had a pretty fair time yourself over the weekend.'

Chopper shrugged.

'Yeah, it wasn't a bad run,' he muttered. 'Plenty of action, plenty of screwing.'

Garman leered at him.

'Yeah - I heard.' His face clouded over for a second. 'What brings you over here, Man? You got the rest of the boys outside?'

Chopper threw his arm around Garman's shoulder in a conspiratorial fashion.

'Wanted to have a little word with you, feller,' he murmured casually. 'Want a beer?'

Mike Garman was grinning stupidly. That Chopper should have come over especially to see him was something really special.

'Thanks, Man.'

Chopper ordered another pint and pulled Garman gently by the arm.

'Let's go and have a quiet chat,' he said, gesturing over to a comparatively quiet corner of the pub.

He led the way across, Garman scurrying happily at his heels.

'So what's all this about, Man?' asked Garman as soon as they had reached the corner. Chopper smiled inwardly as he looked at the kid's face and saw the impatience there. This was going to be easier than he had imagined.

'Got yourself a hog yet?' he inquired casually.

Garman's face fell. 'No, not yet - but it won't be long now.'

Chopper nodded understandably.

'You really ought to get a move on,' he said. 'You're missing out on a hell of a lot of good action.'

The words, and their implication, had the desired effect. Garman's spotty face glowed with pride and elation. Here was Chopper himself, second-in-command to the biggest Angel chapter for miles, actually giving him the green light. Chopper's inference was plain...just as soon as he, Mike Garman, had a hog, he was ready to be taken into the Angels.

Chopper paused to let the words sink in completely. Casually tossing off his beer, he gestured to the counter.

'Want another?'

Garman snatched the glass out of his hand with feverish fingers.

'I'll get 'em Chopper,' he blurted out and ran like a rabbit across to the bar.

When he got back, Chopper was ready to spread jam on the bread and butter.

'Come to think of it, I know someone who's trying to get rid of a really nice hog at the moment,' he mentioned conversationally. 'Poor bastard's really desperate for bread, and he's willing to take half what the bike's worth. Reckon if you had fifty or sixty quid handy you could pick it up.'

Garman's eyes nearly bulged out of his head as he swallowed the ploy hook line and sinker.

'What sort of hog is it?' he wanted to know.

'Norton - stripped down to basics, plating all round and a fibreglass tank. It's a nice hog,' he repeated for effect.

Garman whistled appreciatively.

'You really reckon I could pick it up for fifty quid?' he said in awe.

Chopper nodded.

'Yeah - I reckon so...particularly if I said you was a friend of mine.'

Garman's eyes were shining like searchlight beams.

'Hey - I got that much already,' he blurted happily. 'I was reckoning I'd need a hundred at least.'

'You would,' agreed Chopper, 'But, like I said, this guy needs bread fast to pay for an abortion.'

Mike Garman wasn't really listening any more. In his mind, he had already bought the hog and was riding with the Angels on a run into violence, sex and thrills. He could hear the throbbing sound of engines in his ears and feel the vibration of the bike under his crotch. Birds were running after him, pleading to be picked up and taken on the pillion. He'd have so many women he could say goodbye to wanking for life.

The dream faded as a sudden thought clouded over his mind. His face fell.

'How about getting me initiated, though?' he asked. 'Big M's pretty tough on letting anyone in, ain't he?'

Chopper's eyes narrowed.

'I shouldn't worry about that too much if I were you, Mike,' he said pointedly. 'Won't be any hassle at all if things go the way I plan 'em.'

Garman looked at him piercingly. He saw a catch coming up.

'Something's up,' he said slyly, just catching on to the fact that the world wasn't doing him especial favours that night. 'What is it?'

For a moment, Chopper balked. Once he trusted a miserable little bastard like Garman, there would be no possible way out.

This was the point of no return - for Chopper, for Marty, for Elaine, for all of them. At this moment in time, Chopper had to pull a switch which turned on a machine...and the machine couldn't be switched off again.

Chopper looked at Garman coldly for a few seconds, then pulled the switch.

'I could do with a little bit of help from you and your boys,' said Chopper.

Garman's eyes narrowed to slits.

'What you want - fistpower, or are you pulling a job?' he wanted to know.

Chopper paused to assemble his thoughts, then launched into his spiel.

'Listen, Man - big M is all washed up as an Angel, see. He's got no head for kicks any more, and he's got no guts for action. There've got to be changes. I want the Hells Angels to stay the way they are, not turn into some backstreet motorcycle club for little boys. People like you and me, Mike...WE know what it's about. Big M is getting too old to even remember. Now to work this right, I need your help. Afterwards, when I come out on top, I'll be the one who says who comes in and who goes out of the Angels.'

Garman nodded his head thoughtfully.

'I scratch your back and you'll scratch mine, eh?'

'More or less.'

Garman's ratty little face twitched nervously. This was big league stuff and he felt out of his depth. Big M was a pretty big enemy to tackle. Garman was scared, but the lure Chopper had dangled in front of him was stronger than fear. Bravado won the day.

'OK - what do you want me to do?' he asked.

Chopper breathed an inward sigh of relief. For a while, he had been afraid that Garman wouldn't buy the goods he was selling.

'First of all,' said Chopper. 'I want Big M's bike off the road for a few days. I want him out of action while I get the boys together.'

'What do you want me to do about it?' asked Garman nervously. He didn't fancy tangling personally with Marty Gresham.

'I don't know...anything,' said Chopper irritably. 'Dump sugar in his tank...cement...anything. Drill a hole in the sump, slash the tyres, pinch it...I don't mind, so long as Marty can't ride that hog for a couple of days.'

'Why don't you do it yourself?' Garman wanted to know.

'Don't be a cunt,' snapped Chopper. 'How do you think the other guys would feel if I did it? I got to play it cool, man...be well out of the way when anything's going on. Anyway, I got other things to attend to.'

'When?' queried Garman.

Chopper nibbled nervously at the inside of his mouth.

'Anytime, I guess,' he said. 'The sooner the better. You know Marty's hog...you know where he usually parks it out-side the Greek's. No-one's gonna come looking for you there, because he always makes sure the hog is out of sight.'

Garman considered the scheme carefully for a few more seconds. 'OK,' he snapped at last. 'Leave it to me.'

Chopper downed his drink and turned to leave.

One last thing,' he said as an afterthought. 'If you let me down, Man, I'll fall on you like a ton of shit.'

Garman took the warning to heart.

'Leave it to me,' he repeated grimly. 'Big M won't be able to ride in your victory parade.'

'Be seeing you...Angel,' said Chopper as he left the pub.

Mike Garman's face flushed with pride.

Elaine's heart sank as she heard the familiar sound. Rushing to the window she looked down into the street. Sure enough, it was Marty's hog, throbbing quietly. He sat still, staring up at her window.

'Get down here,' he yelled at her.

A cold lump settled in Elaine's throat. She could tell from the tone of his voice that he was madder than Hell. Worse, she knew how bad he could get.

She cursed herself for a fool. It had been stupid to go to the window and show herself. Maybe he would have assumed she had gone to bed, and not bothered to come up. Now she was trapped, and it seemed that a confrontation was inevitable.

She had been incredibly stupid these last two days. She should have cooled things off gently, gradually, giving Marty no reason to suspect that anything was amiss.

Yet his arms around her had become unbearable. His lips looked unclean when he tried to kiss her. She had been given a choice, and she had taken her pick. She had jumped in feet first with Chopper, and wanted to take the full consequences.

Elaine gathered herself together, took a deep breath, and walked down the stairs to meet Marty.

'You'd better come in,' she called from the front door.

Marty switched off his engine and dismounted. He followed her up the stairs to her room quietly.

'I told you I wasn't feeling very well,' started Elaine defensively. There was always the chance that this was no more than a social call.

'You've told me a lot of shit in the last couple of days,' muttered Marty coldly, and Elaine slumped resignedly into an armchair. His eyes, and tone of voice finally told her that this was the showdown.

'What do you mean?' she asked, wanting to prise out of him exactly what he knew, or suspected.

Marty didn't speak. Instead, he walked slowly across the room towards her and stood over her silently. Suddenly, with the speed of a snake striking, his hand cracked down across the side of her face. Elaine whimpered with pain.

'You know exactly what I mean,' said Marty, flatly. 'You and Chopper.'

There didn't seem to be much point in bluffing, but Elaine tried it anyway.

'I don't know what you mean,' she said defiantly.

Marty's hand crashed down once more across her cheek, bringing tears to her eyes. He reached behind her head, grasping a thick handful of hair and pulled down viciously. Elaine screamed.

'Don't try to fuck me about, babe,' snarled Marty nastily. 'I want the truth and I want it right now.' He finished his words with another hard twist of her hair.

'Marty - you must be out of your head,' Elaine stammered bravely, serving only to inflame him even more. He released her hair, picking only one little bunch of strands between his finger and thumb. With a savage tug, he pulled them out of her head.

'You're gonna be bald unless you start talking soon,' he threatened.

The tears were running freely down Elaine's face now, and her scalp felt as though it were on fire. Marty wound his fingers round another few strands of hair and started to pull on them slowly.

'All right you bastard, I'll tell you,' spat Elaine. 'Whatever you think, then it's yes, yes, yes...and ten times more.'

Marty released his hold, moved slowly back from her and sagged down into another chair. Even while he had been hurting her, there had been a faint hope in his heart that she might deny everything. Now, with her admission, he felt drained, emptied, cold. Even his anger seemed to have evaporated.

'Why?' he muttered eventually.

Elaine sneered at him in derision.

'Because I'm an Angel's girl, that's why,' she said. 'And Big Marty Gresham ain't an Angel anymore. He's nothing.'

'And you think Chopper is it now, do you?'

'Yeah. That's exactly what I think. He's got more guts and fire than you ever had. He ain't afraid to get what he wants - to take it, if need be. Chopper belongs with the Angels...he's a natural leader. You aren't fit to run a kid's playground any more.'

Marty laughed at her coldly.

'And you think you two can just smoothly walk in and take everything away from me? You think Big M is going to give up without a fight?'

Elaine stared at him calmly. 'The fighting's over, Marty. You've already lost. Just give in gracefully, sneak away and open up a tobacconists shop,' she sneered.

Rage boiled up inside Marty once again. He leapt up and ran across the room towards her. Elaine tried to bury her head under her arms to protect herself from the rain of blows which showered down on her. Marty's hand rose again and again in the air, to sweep down across the side of her head, her face, her neck. Only when he was exhausted did he stop, move backwards slowly and walk towards the door.

Elaine lay collapsed on the floor, sobbing uncontrollably.

Marty paused at the door and looked back at her.

'If you think you've been hurt, just wait until your boyfriend gets his,' he said coldly. 'Chopper's going to get a stomping that'll make him wish he had never been born.'

He turned, and walked out.

Elaine heard his hog start up, squeal away from the pavement and fade into the distance as Marty headed for the Greek's.

Nick the Greek never said much, but he thought a lot more than people ever gave him credit for.

CHAPTER THIRTEEN

Right now, Nick was thinking that there was the unmistakable smell of trouble in the air. Big trouble.

He lounged behind the counter, casually wiping cups which had been wiped a dozen times before and watched the small group of Angels sitting in the corner.

Big M, Danny the Deathlover, Freaky, Irish Mick and Max continued their talk, oblivious of Nick's watchful eye. Their voices were low and ominous. Nick tried to listen, but couldn't pick out the words. Eventually, he shrugged to himself and gave up. What his customers did was their concern. It was none of his business.

Sometimes Nick felt that the less he knew, the better he was. That way he never became involved.

Gazing out into the darkening street, Nick noticed a bunch of the Greaser kids hovering about outside, and wondered vaguely if that was where the trouble lay. He hoped not. Gang fights were messy, and he didn't want them happening on his doorstep.

Eventually the Greasers went away, and Nick felt relieved. The council of war continued at the corner table. Nick was convinced that such was the nature of the discussion. He was right.

Back in her room, Elaine gradually recovered herself and managed to stop the racking sobs which had been torturing her for the past half hour. She rose, crossed to the washbasin and wiped the blood and smeared mascara from her face. She dabbed at her bruises gingerly, and hurriedly slapped some make up carelessly on her ravaged face.

She made a strong cup of coffee, and sat down to drink it greedily...and to think.

Somehow, she had to warn Chopper. Perhaps, given enough time, he could think of a way to wriggle out of the trap which at this very minute must be in preparation for him.

Elaine was only too well aware of the nature of Chopper's punishment if he should receive it - and the thought was horrible. A ritual Angel 'stomping' was a rare occurrence - but when it happened, the victim never forgot it. She recalled the last time she had seen such a sentence carried out and shuddered. The kid had spent six weeks in hospital for his crime of grassing to the fuzz, and still bore a five-inch scar from his cheekbone to his chin.

The thought of Chopper's handsome face marred in his way made her shudder again. Frantically, she finished the coffee, threw on some clothes and ran down the stairs to summon a taxi in the street.

She waited impatiently in the street as cars flashed by. Time was so important. She glanced at her watch nervously. It was nine-fifteen.

Hours seemed to drag by until a taxi cruised along the street with a faint yellow light showing at the front. Elaine stepped into the road, waving her hands frantically, and the cab pulled into the kerb.

The journey to Chopper's place took only a few minutes, but to Elaine, it seemed like an eternity.

At last the taxi pulled up outside. Elaine leapt from the cab, bidding the driver to wait for her, She ran up the front path to the porch. She pressed Chopper's bell.

There was no answer. Desperately, Elaine jammed her finger against the small button, as though it could magically produce Chopper out of thin air. She waited another half a minute and walked slowly back to the taxi.

'Frampton Street,' she muttered to the driver in a resigned voice. There seemed no other choice but to go to the Greek's.

Elaine sat back in the taxi and struggled to cope with her worries. Marty would probably be at the Greek's, she thought, and perhaps Chopper had already gone there to walk into his fate. Elaine wasn't sure what she could really do to make any difference to the events of the night, but she knew that she had to try.

'This'll do,' she called to the driver, tapping the glass partition. She recognised the corner of the street which led up to Nick's cafe.

The cab stopped. Elaine paid him, and walked slowly up the dimly lit street towards the Greek's.

She passed the small alleyway where Marty invariably parked his hog and paused. It might be as well to check if he was there. She ducked down the dark alley and turned into a small cul-de-sac. Marty always tucked his hog out of the way...he was too scared that it presented an irresistible target to roaming Skinheads.

As she walked down the cul-de-sac, she looked ahead and started. There was Marty's hog all right - propped up against the wall, but there were shadowy figures bending over it. As she looked, a blurred face looked up and saw her.

There was a rapid murmur of voices, and the sound of something metallic rattling to the ground. The shadowy figures moved rapidly, scurrying away from the hog to jump over a low fence which offered the only escape route from the blind alley.

Elaine waited for them to make good their escape before walking on. She approached the parked hog and looked over it carefully. In the darkness, it was difficult to see much at all. Her feet struck something on the ground, which scraped along with a sound of metal on stone.

Elaine bent down to pick up the small hacksaw. She stared at it with incomprehension for a few seconds, before realisation struck her. Kneeling on the ground, she struck a match and examined the frame of the hog carefully.

A small pile of metal filings on the ground led her to the damage. On the underside of the main frame, the saw-cut went deep...almost half-way through the thick tubing.

Garman and his boys had been true to their word. If they had been given time to finish the job, Marty's hog would have been rendered completely useless. With the main frame sawn through, the entire front of the hog would have collapsed, necessitating a lengthy and major repair job.

Elaine had no idea who the saboteurs had been, but automatically assumed that Chopper had arranged it. She smiled grimly to herself. Chopper was a good thinker. Without his hog, Big M was reduced to virtually nothing.

She continued staring at the damaged bike thoughtfully, wondering what to do. The cut went deep enough to render the bike extremely dangerous. It would be only a matter of time before the tubing sheared through and the frame collapsed.

Elaine's mouth tightened into a grim line as she recalled the beating-up she had suffered at Marty's hands. With a savage smile, she hurled the hacksaw over the nearest fence, and scuffed the shiny metal filings with her foot, mixing them into the dust. Just to make sure, she ran her fingers along the bottom of the frame until they were thick with dirt and black grease. She rubbed it carefully into the saw-cut, camouflaging the shiny glitter of the raw metal.

Elaine stood up, wiped her hands on the side of her jeans and stood back to admire her handiwork. The hog looked completely normal - only a very careful inspection would reveal that there was anything wrong.

Satisfied, Elaine turned away and walked slowly up the alley towards the Greek's.

Inside, the group sitting in the corner had grown. Pretty Boy Parritt and Screwball Sam had arrived, been informed of the situation and had vowed their solidarity with Big M.

Nick, still wiping the same cups, saw Elaine through the window.

'Hey,' he called out to Marty. 'You can cheer up now...your girlfriend's arrived.'

Big M flashed his eyes quickly at Danny the Deathlover in an unspoken sign. The plans had been made, every possible move covered. Silently, Danny and Freaky stood up and headed for the door.

They reached Elaine before she entered the cafe.

'You ain't going in there, babe,' muttered Danny, grabbing her arm. 'We're all going for a nice little ride.'

Elaine struggled to free herself. Freaky gripped her other arm and pulled her away from the door.

'Is Chopper in there?' she managed to blurt out.

Danny grinned.

'No, not yet,' he said. 'But I expect he'll be along soon. Big M doesn't like to be kept waiting too long. Meanwhile, we're all going to take a ride, and they'll meet us later.'

Freaky leered at her.

'Big M kinda thought you'd be along,' he said. 'Reckoned you might like to take one last look at Chopper while he still has a face.'

Elaine struggled violently, but it was no use. She gave up, and allowed them to drag her away from the cafe to where the hogs were parked.

'Get on,' snapped Freaky, gesturing to his pillion seat.

'Where are you taking me?' Elaine whimpered in a frightened voice.

'Wanstead Flats,' said Danny. 'Don't fuck around and you won't get hurt.'

Elaine meekly obeyed, and climbed on the back of Freaky's hog. He started it up, and pulled slowly away.

Big M stared through the window of the cafe after them and grinned savagely. So she wanted kicks, did she? Well tonight she was going to get them...and she was gong to learn that Big Marty Gresham was far from soft. He called Nick over to the table.

'Five teas, Nick.'

He relaxed in his chair waiting for Chopper.

Chopper dipped one finger into the pool of slopped beer on the pub counter. He drew wet, squiggly spiders as he wondered what to do.

A couple of hours had passed since he had spoken to Mike Garman. Since then, he had ridden over to Dagenham in search of Ethel and his boys without success. Now he was cruising about aimlessly, stopping in various pubs to choke down another pint.

With a sudden burst of decision, he picked up his glass and downed his sixth pint of the night. There was nothing else to do than go to the Greek's. If Marty was there, too bad...and if he wasn't, then maybe Chopper could start pulling the boys over to his side.

He walked outside to his hog, kicked it into life and headed for the Greek's.

The fates were converging, circumstances were meshing together into a tangled web and time was running out for everyone as he sped towards the little cafe.

Chopper walked through the door, and gave his customary grin to Nick. He glanced around, seeing the group of Angels tucked in the corner, and moved towards them.

It was a weird tableau - made up of actors who didn't really want to take part, and had not chosen their roles willingly. Instead, they accepted the action for what it was, falling meekly into line with the quirk of the scriptwriter who had thrown them all together on this small stage.

Big M looked up as Chopper approached and forced a welcoming smile onto his face. The others had been carefully briefed - Chopper was to suspect nothing. Tonight was a night just like any other.

'Hi Chop,' said Marty, still smiling.

Chopper glanced at the ring of faces, saw nothing in them and relaxed. Only Nick, the uninterested observer, sensed the full degree of tension in the air.

'Nothing much...as you can see,' said Big M calmly. 'We was just talking about digging up some action tonight.'

'Yeah? What sort of action?'

Irish Mick grinned pleasantly. 'Big M was just suggesting we shoot over and do a bit of Paki-bashing,' he said. 'Over in Stratford.'

Chopper nodded his head agreeably.

'Sounds like fun,' he said. 'No one else around?'

Big M shook his head.

'Nope...things is pretty quiet.'

Chopper smiled. A bit of real action was just what he wanted right now. He welcomed the chance of working off some of his inner frustrations on a few Pakistanis and Indians.

'Well, what are we waiting for?' he asked, and stood up. Big M and the rest of the boys followed him.

Chopper kicked over his bike and waited for Marty to go and collect his. As he reappeared in front of the Greek's, the riders set off - down through Dalston until they came to the Mile End Road, and then a straight run over the Stratford flyover and up the Romford Road.

Big M led the field, with Chopper close behind him and the rest bringing up the rear.

Turning off at Stratford Broadway, Big M led the way down the Romford Road as far as the Princess Alice, and turned left into Woodgrange Road.

Chopper started to feel the faintest misgivings as he followed Marty up through Forest Gate. This wasn't a Paki area, he thought - most of the blacks lived back towards East Ham and Stratford.

The road led directly on to the wild expanse of Wanstead Flats. Chopper started to feel really worried. Now he was almost sure that something was up. For a second, he thought of turning his hog round in the road and making a run for it.

Then he realised that Irish Mick and Pretty Boy were right on his tail and the pieces of the jigsaw started to fit together.

He was trapped. he had walked right into it with his eyes open. The only thing he could do now was to keep his cool, and hope for the best.

Marty signalled them to slow down and pulled off the main road onto the grass verge. He pointed across the empty, deserted waste land towards the dim shape of the bandstand. Nearby, Chopper could just pick out the faint glow of hog headlights.

Irish Mick, Pretty Boy and Max closed in really tight behind him. Marty turned towards him and there was a wicked grin of triumph on his face.

'Welcome to the party, Chopper,' he said grimly. 'It's all in your honour.'

Motioning the others to follow him Big M scrambled his hog across the grass towards the bandstand.

As they arrived, Chopper saw Elaine, and one glance at her bruised face told him all he wanted to know. Fear gripped in his belly as he looked around at the grim faces of his former friends.

Big M parked his hog, climbed off and swaggered across to Chopper.

'Well, Man,' he said. 'I guess you know what you're here for.'

Chopper fought to control the horde of rats running around in his stomach. Their sharp claws dug painfully into his insides, and their teeth tore out his guts in huge bites.

He stared out across the empty wilderness of the Flats.

'No one around to help you, feller,' murmured Marty, as though reading his thoughts. 'You're all on your own.'

Chopper's eyes flashed towards Danny, who stood staring at him impassively.

'Come on Danny...tell Marty all this is pointless,' he pleaded desperately. 'Stick with me now, and we'll make everyone from here to Golders Green fear the Angels.'

Danny the Deathlover just stared at him silently and sadly, and turned away.

'Mick...Freaky,' screamed Chopper. 'We're friends, remember?'

'We're also Angels, Chopper,' reminded Freaky in a low voice. 'And we live by the rules...all of them.'

Chopper felt the panic rising in his throat as a semi-circle of Angels arranged themselves around him. They moved slowly towards him fists hanging down at their sides.

'For Christ's sake, Marty...leave him alone,' shrieked Elaine, who had been left to watch the scene alone.

Marty turned towards her, slowly. He started at her for several seconds as though wondering what to do. 'Yeah. Come to think of it. I guess you're pretty much to blame,' he murmured distantly. 'Chopper was my friend.'

He jerked a thumb towards her.

'Grab her,' he commanded.

Freaky and Danny ran across to Elaine and pinned her arms behind her back. Marty turned on her, as though forgetting all about Chopper. He walked up to her slowly, one hand outstretched.

Gripping the front of her blouse, he yanked at it viciously. The thin material ripped, exposing her brassiere underneath.

Marty flicked the same hand upwards in a sudden blur of movement. The back of his palm caught her a stinging slap across the side of the face.

Elaine squealed with pain and threw her head back. She sucked in her cheeks and made a rough, coughing sound in her throat. Filling her mouth with phlegm, she spat full in his face.

Marty stood back a moment. Then, he slowly and deliberately raised his hand to wipe the spittle from his face.

'That was silly,' he muttered harshly, and turned back to Chopper.

Chopper fought to get at him, but Screwball Sam and Pretty Boy held him tightly in a vicious neck-hold.

'Here you are, Chopper,' said Marty slowly. 'Here's the bird you wanted so desperately. Why don't you help yourself, Man.'

As he spoke, Marty moved forwards and grabbed hold of Elaine's bra. He tugged at it, and the elastic gave way with a sudden snap.

'Here you are,' Marty went on, gripping one of her breasts in his hand until she screamed out. 'Help yourself to handful of tit...In fact why doesn't everyone help themselves?'

He reached out and pulled Irish Mick by the arm.

'Here, Mick - grab a handful,' he said, pointing to Elaine's breast. 'If it's good enough for Chopper, it's good enough for you.'

Mick hesitated, unsure how to react.

'Come on, Man don't be bashful,' snapped Marty. He grabbed Irish Mick's hand, pressing it on to Elaine's breasts. 'Give 'em a good feel...give 'em a squeeze,' he went on harshly. 'A real beautiful pair, aren't they?'

He turned on the rest of the boys.

'Who else wants a handful?' he asked. 'Who wants to take the chance of a lifetime?'

Danny laughed nervously. Max shifted his feet and tried to look the other way.

'You bastard,' Elaine spat at him. 'Your filthy hands ain't fit to pick up shit.'

Marty's hand smashed across her face once again.

'You got a real mean tongue, babe,' he said calmly. 'Funny I never noticed it before.'

He reached out and pulled her hair, twisting it behind her and pulling it downwards. Elaine fell to the ground in a heap.

'Take her jeans off,' Marty snapped to Irish Mick.

Mick looked at him dubiously for a second, then obeyed meekly. Elaine struggled and kicked as he unfastened the clip and pulled the jeans down over her knees and ankles.

'And the tights,' added Marty.

Elaine lay on the ground, naked. She looked up in fear and horror as Marty fished in the fly of his jeans.

'Hold her down,' he snapped to Irish Mick and Danny. They obeyed blindly. Marty knelt on the grass over her prostrate body.

'Better look as though you're enjoying it,' he said to Elaine with an icy stare. 'You always used to.'

Elaine screamed continuously as Marty raped her savagely. When he was finished, he looked up at Danny.

'Your turn,' he said quietly.

Danny grabbed him by the sleeve.

'Come on, Man...there's no need for this...' he started to protest. Marty cut him short.

'Do it, Man...that's an order,' he repeated coolly.

Danny unzipped himself, and fell upon the still screaming Elaine.

Chopper looked on in horror and fury as each took a turn to defile the helpless Elaine. When the last one had finished, she lay there silently, by now beyond even feeling pain.

Marty stood over her and pulled out his penis once more. He urinated over her prostrate body with a stony look on his face. Not content with this he walked slowly back to his hog and took a can of engine oil out of the toolbox. Uncapping it, he poured the contents over her breasts and stomach, then reached down to roll her over in the dirt.

At last, he was through. He moved away from her wearily.

'OK,' he murmured distantly. 'Take her away and dump her somewhere.' He signalled to Irish Mick and Pretty Boy.

They stepped forward and bent over the unconscious girl and lifted her gently.

Big M turned back to Chopper.

'Now it's your turn, Chop,' he said without anger. 'I guess you have a pretty good idea of what's coming to you.'

Chopper was biting at his lip with panic. Already he had drawn blood, which was dribbling down his chin.

He struggled to think of a bluff which would save him. Bravado was the only thing he had left now.

'Beating up a woman's about the only thing you're good for, Marty,' he said derisively. 'You'd better go and sit down while the boys do the dirty work for you. Hitting me might bruise your soft little knuckles.'

Marty refused to be goaded. He laughed in Chopper's face.

'There ain't anything I can't handle by myself if I choose to,' he stated flatly.

'Yeah?' shouted Chopper, fighting desperately for time and an opportunity. 'Well why don't you show some guts for once in your life and try to handle me on your own?'

'There's no point,' said Marty softly. 'You're an Angel, so you know that breaking faith brings about punishment. You've crossed the others just as much as you've crossed me. Therefore, they have an equal share in your punishment.'

Chopper saw a glimmer of hope through the blackness of his desperation, He turned his attention to the others.

'Listen to this,' he screamed. 'Little Marty Gresham is trying to pull you all in because I screwed his precious bird. He's trying to make you all forget that this is a personal quarrel because he hasn't got the guts to tackle me on his own.'

'That's enough, Chopper,' snapped Marty suddenly. He stepped forwards and smashed his fist into Chopper's nose.

Chopper shook his head to clear the water from his eyes. His arms were still pinioned tightly behind him.

'See what I mean?' he yelled over his shoulder. 'The gutless bastard can't even hit me unless he's got you two holding me back.'

Chopper sensed the grip on his arms weaken slightly, and realised that he had stumbled on his only chance.

'I challenge you, Marty,' he shouted. 'I challenge you openly in front of everyone to prove that you're fit to be an Angel leader. I got a right to a personal challenge - you bloody well know that.'

There was an awkward silence. Finally Danny spoke up nervously.

'He's right you know, Big M,' he murmured in a low voice. 'Chopper's not really done anything to cross the rest of us. He's got a right to challenge you.'

Behind Danny, Irish Mick and Max mumbled their agreement.

Chopper smiled triumphantly.

'How about it, BIG man?' he said tauntingly.

Marty glared at him silently in sullen anger.

'OK then,' said Marty as Chopper walked towards him. 'Let's see what you can do.' He brandished his fists up in front of his face.

Chopper stopped a few feet away.

'Just the two of us, Marty,' he said in a soft voice. 'We were friends once...remember? I think it would be better for both of us if we were on our own. Either way this ends up, one of us is going to be shown up...and perhaps it would be better if there were no eye-witnesses.'

Marty thought for a second.

'Yeah - maybe you're right,' he admitted grudgingly. 'The rest of you guys head on back to the Greek's. I'll join you later.'

'Just a minute, fellers,' said Chopper, seizing hold of his advantage, 'There's two possible ways this fight will end. Maybe it'll be ME strolling back to the Greek's afterwards...If that's so, I guess Marty would be the first one to admit that I'd proved myself top man...right, Big M?'

'Right,' Marty snapped.

'And so this little bundle is for the big stakes, right? If you beat me, I leave the Angels. If I win, I take over?'

'OK,' said Marty wearily. 'This one is the big one.'

Danny and the rest of the boys drifted back to their hogs. Marty and Chopper stood silently facing one another as the bikes roared off across the Flats.

'Anytime you're ready,' muttered Marty, circling round Chop-per warily.

'Yeah - I'm ready,' gritted Chopper, and swung his booted

foot upwards in a vicious arc towards Marty's groin. Marty side-stepped quickly, avoiding the blow.

'Want to play it without rules, do you man?' asked Marty with a wry grin and lunged forward with his head tucked down.

Chopper wasn't expecting the sudden butt. The top of Marty's head crunched into his nose with a sickening thud.

Chopper felt the warm taste of blood as it trickled down his nose into the corners of his mouth.

He danced away from Marty's weaving figure, his hand busy behind his back. He fished in his back pocket and his fingers closed around a heavy piece of chain.

Whipping it out suddenly, he swung it wildly in the direction of Marty's face. Marty jumped back hurriedly - but not quite fast enough. The end of the chain caught him just above the eye, tearing a large lump of his eyebrow away.

Marty snatched at the heavy chain hanging around his neck. Pulling it savagely, it snapped and came away, complete with the heavy iron Nazi cross which decorated it. He whirled the evil weapon in the air.

Chopper looked at it and ducked back fast. If one corner of that cross caught him, it could slash his face like a razor.

He waited his moment to strike again with the chain...and saw it. As Marty moved forwards, Chopper stepped sideways quickly and came up on him from an unguarded angle. He smashed the heavy bike chain down on Marty's wrist. The cross and chain fell out of his numbed fingers.

Chopper made sure he didn't lose the advantage. While Marty was still rattled, he lunged forward, and brought his heavy boot up hard into Marty's balls. Marty doubled up with pain and started to sink to the ground.

Chopper jumped round behind him and smashed the chain down on the back of his neck. As Marty collapsed, Chopper raised his arm again and again, raining blow after blow on top of Marty's unprotected head. Chopper kept smashing the chain down until his arm was exhausted.

Marty lay unconscious, a pool of blood trickling out of his hair.

Chopper stood back to catch his breath and stared at him for a while. For a moment, he thought Marty was dead, but then he saw his chest move gently. He was still breathing.

Chopper spat on to Marty's body and walked slowly and painfully towards his hog. Despite his pain and fatigue, he felt happy. He had won...he had proved himself. He had gained victory and established himself at the top of the pile where he belonged.

He climbed on his bike and kicked it over...then suddenly changed his mind.

No, he thought with a sudden flash of inspiration. A leader should ride a leader's hog. he switched off his engine and strolled over to Marty's Harley-Davidson.

He sat astride the hog proudly, kicking it into life and marvelling at the feel of real power under his legs.

Now he could ride back to the Greeks in triumph...home like a conquering hero on his captured trophy.

He pulled across the flats onto the main road.

Down the Romford Road, he gunned the engine, surging with elation as the powerful hog responded to him as though it was part of his being.

The Mile End Road loomed up, along that and Chopper passed under the Stratford flyover.

A slow, stupid grin spread across his face. What better time than to prove the one thing he really wanted to...that he was a better rider than Marty had ever been?

Now, he had the hog...and he had the opportunity. His mind made up, Chopper slowed down at the intersection, and did a U-turn to take him into the opposite carriageway.

He pulled back the throttle and headed for the flyover like a cross bow bolt.

The hog screamed up the approach slope. Chopper glanced down at the speedo and saw it quivering at around that magical 100 mark. He was going to do it...he was going to smash Marty's record.

The hog reached the apex of the flyover and the front suspension bit down into the tarmac. The hydraulics hit rock bottom, and hit back, plunging the telescopic forks back up to add impetus to the upward movement of the bike.

The front wheels cleared the air, and Chopper felt once again that glorious sensation of flying.

The wheels were dead in line as he came down a split second later. The forks absorbed most of the shock and transferred it into the frame.

...The weakened frame.

It was too much strain. The tubing buckled and sheared with the shock. The frame collapsed, the forks twisted at a strange angel by the forces pulling at the hog.

Chopper didn't even have time to wipe the triumphant smile from his face as he plunged head first into the road and smashed open his skull.

He was dead before the front wheel stopped spinning.